# CIRCLES

Heather Jornay Perkins

Black Access
Granted
Dallas, Texas

**Black Access Granted**
PO Box 172176
Dallas, Texas 75217
Visit our website at www.blackaccessgranted.com
Visit Author website at www.heatherjperkins.com

The characters and events portrayed in this book are fictitious. Any similarity to real persons, living, or dead, is coincidental and not intended by the author.

Circles: a novel / by Heather Jornay Perkins.

1st Circles Edition

Printed in the United States of America

10 9 8 7 6 5 4 3 2 1

## Dédicace

God has blessed me with the gift to put creativity on paper; that's more than a virtue. Before I started the creation of this book, I asked myself one question, *What are other authors not writing about*. I thought long and hard about a possible answer; then it hit me. The answer was that it's not what others are writing or not writing about; it's simply the person holding the pen. I'd like to first thank God for giving me the strength, the will, and the vision. I'd like to thank my mother, Darlene Johnson, for always pushing me and encouraging me to not allow anyone to stop me from accomplishing my goals. My father, Michael Spillman, for believing in all the things I've ever wanted to achieve. Love you both so much. Thanks to all of my 6 brothers, Aunt Mary, Michael Watson, Michael Polk, Jonathan Mouton, and Tyrone Samples. All of these people helped and pushed me to never quit writing. Special hugs and kisses to my two sons Michael and Anthone' Watson for being my inspiration. Praising God is a habit for me and that's a habit that I will not break. I love you God, I love myself, I love my sons, and I love my gift to write and being able to share my writings with others. Thanks to all of the readers out there and especially to the ones who will read this book.

# CONTENTS

# CIRCLES

Circles

## 1. AN OLD FRIEND

AS VANN WALKED to the front door of his apartment, he noticed an envelope taped to his door. The first thing that came to his mind was that it was a late notice from the rent office as he was a little behind on this month's rent. He pulled the envelope off the door and noticed that it didn't say anything on the outside of it besides 'OPEN'. As he read the words, he could not escape the sweet scent of perfume flowing from it into his nostrils. The scent was familiar but he couldn't put his finger on where he smelled the scent before. 'OPEN', Vann wondered who the note could have come from.

Vann unlocked his door, walked into his apartment, and closed the door quickly while still staring at the note intrigued. He locked the door and took a seat on the couch. Vann was exhausted, so he laid his head back and placed his hand on his forehead then closed his eyes. Who would have thought that being a construction site manager would drain you of so much energy?

He opened his eyes and raised his head to stare at the envelope a few more seconds before he finally unsealed it. He was shocked to see who it was from. It was a note from an old friend, Chenelle. Chenelle was a young lady that Vann once had a relationship with. They were really close and shared a lot together. One could say that she was the love of his life; until she left him to pursue her education and career. Vann was hurt and, for a while, he refused to open his heart up and let another woman in. That was until he met Trese. Now Trese carried him through the hurt and gave him a chance to love again, and so he grabbed on to the opportunity.

The note was very short and to the point:

*Thursday-March 28, 2008*
*Baby, I just thought you should know that your girl is back in town for a few weeks on business and I really would like*

*to see you again and spend some time together if possible. Sorry I came by unannounced, but I just couldn't help myself. Besides, your number has changed and I didn't know any other way to get in touch with you. I need to talk to you so please call me: (713) 555-4278.*

*Yours forever,*
*Ms. Chenelle Jones*

After reading Chenelle's note, Vann's tiredness turned into a rush of excitement; he was very anxious to see her. Vann couldn't believe his girl was back in town and she thought of a brother. Vann needed a place to stash the note, so he stuffed it inside a pair of his old Jordans that he hadn't worn in a minute. But knowing Trese, she would probably find it anyway. But man, just the thought of Chenelle was worth the risk.

Chenelle was this sexy ass chic that was hard to forget about. Her skin was a smooth, light caramel complexion. Her hair was sandy brown, long, and straight. Her lips were nice and superb. Her eyes were an astonishing hazel chestnut color and her body was; well, she had curves in all the right places. Chenelle was the classy, business, but ghetto type and she knew how to please her man in the bedroom. After a moment of deep reflection of her, all Vann could say to himself was, *DAMN! I must be that nigga, huh.*

This news was so damn good to him that he had to hit his boy Darren up. Vann and Darren practically grew up together and had been boys since high school. They both worked for DMV Construction and each had worked their way up to management. They were running mates both on and off the job.

Vann called Darren to tell him about Chenelle's note. "Nigga! You better call her! A woman leaving an unexpected note on your front door either means she wants some or she has something important to tell you," Darren told him.

"Dang! Aight big homie. I'ma call her and see what tha biz is," Vann replied.

"Aight, just holla at me," Darren told him.

"Aight bro. I'ma hit you up in a min," Vann said before clicking him off of the line.

# Circles

After Vann hung up with Darren, he called Chenelle. Although he was nervous, his fingers moved quickly to dial her number. He sweated with anticipation as the dead air prepared to play a ring tone. The phone rang a couple of times then a sweet voice answered, "Yes, this is Chenelle." After he started blabbering, he noticed that it was just Chenelle's voicemail, so he waited for the beep and then left her a message.

"Yeah, this ya boy V. You came by earlier and I got your little note, cute. Hit me back, cutie."

Chenelle was sitting right by her phone. She usually didn't answer unfamiliar numbers so she decided to let the caller go to voicemail. Sitting alone in her hotel room at the Sheraton, she turned the volume down on the television and then picked up her phone to check her voicemail. She was very surprised to hear Vann's voice. She smiled and hurried to return his call.

Vann had the shower going and the steam was fogging up the mirror. Just as he was about to drop his boxers and step in, his phone rang. He checked the caller id and noticed it was Chenelle calling him back. He rushed out of the bathroom and into his bedroom with a smile so big that it could have lasted for days. He answered the phone, "What's good with ya mami?"

"What's good? Well, how about you and me, that's if you're not spoken for," Chenelle said while laughing.

"Hey I like the sound of that! Yeah, that was a cute note you left me. I really wasn't expecting it from you tho. I can't believe you actually thought about me," Vann told her.

"Hmmm. Well, yeah of course. Why wouldn't I? So, what's been up with you?" she asked him.

"Not much since you left. I'm still at DMV; I'm a site manager now," Vann replied with pride.

"Wow! Really! Congrats!" she responded.

"Yeah and that's going good for me. And I have one more semester left at UNT. It was a slow process, but I'm in the home stretch now. And…I am spoken for," Vann ended with a bang.

"You have a woman? Oh so that explains the number change. That's great you're a manager now and still with the same company, and wow last semester at school! I'm happy to hear that!" Chenelle recapped to him.

"So what have you been up to?" Vann asked her now engaging her about her happenings.

"Well, I'm still living in Houston and as you should already know I have another semester left in school and then I will be heading to law school in Mississippi. I'm still making money, no kids, and I have my guy friends who I kick it with every now and then. Well, that's whenever I have the time."

"Hmmm. Your guy friends. So how many do you have?" he asked her.

"Oh, a good girl never tells," she told him while laughing. Vann laughed too but he was serious. He really wanted to know. "So how is your commitment with your girl?" Chenelle asked.

"My commitment with her is how it should be. We have been together for about a year now," Vann answered.

"Oh, ok. A year, wow! Well, enough of that. When can I see you?" Chenelle asked him.

Vann didn't quickly respond back. He paused for a moment and thought about when he would actually have the time. "Damn! Let me call you back with that one and I will let you know, since I am taken now. If that's ok?" Vann asked Chenelle.

"Yeah, you can. But don't have me waiting too long." Chenelle was coming on to Vann a little strong. But it was just so she could see if he still had a thing for her.

"Aight then, let me call you back," Vann said before he hung up the phone. After hanging up with her, he got in the shower with a lot on his mind. He couldn't wait to see Chenelle, but he had to get around Trese first. He had to make sure his girl never found out.

After Van got out of the shower, Trese arrived knocking at the door. "Yeah, who is it?" Vann shouted while he was still drying off.

"It's me baby," Trese yelled. Vann wrapped his towel around his waist and went to open up the door for her. When he opened it, Trese had a big smile on her face as she looked him up and down. She walked in and closed the door behind her, while pulling Vann close to her. Vann then asked what was wrong with her.

# Circles

"Oh, nothing I'm just happy to see my man; especially in nothing but a towel," Trese said as she pulled him even closer. Trese embraced him with a hug and a kiss on the cheek, "Ummm, I miss my baby."

"Oh yeah!" Vann said.

"Uh, huh. I've missed you all day," Trese told him. Vann picked Trese up and laid her on the couch. He started kissing her gently on the neck and then aggressively in the mouth. He rubbed her body while he kissed her constantly. Trese then felt an urging sensation making her want him even more. The passion between them arose leading to fulfillment of lovemaking.

Trese was nothing like Chenelle; she was the total opposite. Trese had a light brown-skinned complexion. Her hair was short and she kept it up in the tightest hairstyles that money could buy. Her eyes were a light brownish color and she was a thick girl, although not too thick. Her body was just the right size to show off her curves in all the right places. She was 5'3 and was not the bourgeois type at all. Trese was a real woman and kept it real with her man; at least that's what she always claimed her motto to be.

After all the kissing and rubbing, Vann and Trese had amazing sex on the couch. The sex was so driven that they both fell asleep in each other's arms. While asleep, Trese's phone kept ringing and her text messages kept coming through. Trese finally picked up the phone and saw that it was her girl, Peaches. She declined her call because she was spending quality time with her man and she really didn't want any interruptions.

Still half asleep, Vann asked her who kept calling her?

"Nobody but Peaches. I just left her at work. What does she want now?!" Trese said sounding frustrating.

"You alright baby?" Vann asked her with concern.

"Yes, baby I'm okay," she said in a soft tone.

Vann pulled her back to his side and held her close. His eyes were still closed and his arms were gripped tightly around her.

Chenelle had just finished sipping on some Blackberry Alize as she completed one of her cases she was conducting researching for. She just couldn't stop thinking about Vann.

She and Vann had a special thing going on back in the day and they fell in love. But the different lifestyles they lived just wouldn't allow them to come together on a deeper level. She sat in a daze and thought about the last time she saw him and the last time they had sex. They had such a miraculous sex life that the thoughts started making her feel even more vulnerable than she was before. She was so vulnerable that she had to take a hot, steamy bubble bath to soothe her body from the warm sensation she was feeling between her thighs.

As she undressed herself and stepped into the hot water, she finally felt relaxed enough to think of a game plan to tell Vann the truth. If nothing else, she wanted to at least get close to him so she could tell him what she was feeling. Her intensions were to take care of her personal business with Greedy and to reconnect with Vann. Vann was not aware, but she really based her decision on moving to Houston because he hurt her when they were together.

Vann wasn't a perfect man. He did some things that she just couldn't understand and he was driving her crazy. After supposedly loving her and then having the most passionately intense sex with her, *BOOM*, there was always a woman after every woman. Yes, Vann was a male hoe. He never admitted to it, but the truth was always there. Chenelle used to think that he was just addicted to women and sex. It got to the point to where she began to think *what man wouldn't be a hoe because that was the main point of being a man,* right? After all this time, she was still hurt by the way he treated her and her hurt and anger made her want to seek revenge on him. After the thinking and the plotting, Chenelle relaxed a little bit more and then finished up some work that she had brought with her from the office.

Trese and Vann finally got up from their cuddling moment. Trese dressed and then left to go to her place while Vann got ready to go to the gym to workout. Trese couldn't wait to check her text messages. As expected, Peaches didn't want anything but to gossip. Peaches left her a message saying to call her. Trese decided not to call her until she made it to her place. Besides, she had two more messages to check; a text and a voice message. She called her voicemail and it was Tremaine, "Hey, what's up baby girl? I know you see me calling your punk ass! Hit me up when you get this aight!"

Tremaine was an old friend of Trese's. He was a guy friend who she could call on in her time of need or for just whatever. The text message was from Tremaine too. He was asking where she was at. He was acting like he really wanted to see Trese because he was calling and texting her like crazy. On her drive home, she texted Tremaine and told him that she was on her way to her place. He replied back, saying to call him when she made it there. Trese stopped by Williams Chicken to get her something to eat before she made it to the house.

She lived in the North part of Dallas, just down the street from Vann. Trese pulled into her apartment complex, parked, and then went inside. She placed her food on the counter in the kitchen and then went to her room. She plopped on her bed, took her shoes off and then slipped into something more comfortable, her boxers and a tank top. After she changed, she went back into the kitchen, washed her hands, and then grabbed her food. Before she started to eat, she sat down on her couch, in the living room, and turned the television on BET. She then called Tremaine. "Now, where your punk ass at?"

"Nah nigga, where you at?" he asked her while smiling.

"I'm at home," she told him.

"Oh, ok. Well, let me take care of this business real fast and I'll hit you up when I'm on my way," he told her.

"Oh, ok. Make sure you bring me some of that medicine too!" Trese said.

"Aight, I got you," he said.

"And hurry up too, Tremaine. You know how you get sometimes." Trese couldn't wait to see Tremaine. She hadn't seen him in a while. It had actually been since the beginning of the New Year so it was time to see him and catch up.

After hanging up with him, she finished up her food and then called Peaches to see what was up with her.

VANN PULLED INTO the parking lot of LA Fitness where he met up with his boys Darren and Greedy. Darren pulled up on the side of Vann in his 2007 Cadillac CTS sitting on 24's, painted camillionaire blue, with the blue and white interior, and his name embedded in the seats. Vann had a 2007

Yukon Denali with the Burgundy frost paint and the same color interior. He had black limo tint and 26's with the flat screens in the back of the headrests. Greedy pulled up just a little after Darren did. His car was nice. He had an old school 2-door cutlass with a burnt orange color and gold flakes in the paint. He had gold 22's and the interior was burnt orange and white. From the looks of their rides, you would assume they were all dope dealers. But Vann and Darren left that up to Greedy. Greedy was all about getting his paper and winning the competition. He owned three cars and ran two trap houses that kept his pockets fat.

"What's up boy?" Vann said while stepping out of the Yukon. He slapped hands with Darren.

"What up nigga!" Darren said.

"Look at this nigga!" Vann said while pointing at Greedy. Greedy had the volume of his music turned up to the highest notch and a blunt still in his mouth all while he was still puffing. Bobbing his head to his music, he grinned and showed off his grill. He was being his usual self, a show off.

He finally turned his car off, and jumped out, "What up D! You ready for the gym V?" Greedy asked Vann, slapping hands with him and Darren.

"Yeah, I was born ready. You know I can't stay away from the gym," Vann said.

Grabbing their gym bags out of their trunks, Darren asked Vann if he had called Chenelle back. Vann gave him a quick inside peep about he and Chenelle's conversation. After they got their bags, they headed into the fitness center talking loud, playing around, and not caring who was looking or listening. All three of them always liked to be the center of attention, especially Greedy. Vann, Darren, and Greedy were the best of friends. They were each as different as night and day, but all three of them kept it hood.

After working out, Darren and Greedy left but Vann stayed there a little while longer. He did a few more chest presses and then sat on a bench in a daze. Vann sat there thinking of the times he spent with Chenelle. He sat in a daze for so long that he didn't realize how late it was and that the fitness center was about to close. He gathered his things and headed towards his car. Right when he was about to pull off, he received a text message from Trese saying that she was going to bed because she had to get up earlier than usual the next morning. Of course, Vann didn't think anything of it. He just texted her back and said that that was cool with him. He was tired anyway from working out with her and at the fitness center. But Trese was not at all about to call it quits. She had Tremaine over and they were kicking it big, just like she didn't have a man.

"Damn, baby this some good shit right?" Tremaine asked Trese while handing her the blunt.

"Yeah it is," she said.

"So, you couldn't answer your phone because you were with that nigga, huh?" he asked her.

"Boy! Don't be asking me that shit! You know I don't discuss my man and what we do with your ass!" Trese was going off on Tremaine.

"Aight, baby. Calm down. I was just making sure you were straight," Tremaine told her as he rubbed on her thighs, sitting right next to her on the couch.

Tremaine always wanted more from Trese, but Trese was in love with Vann and she didn't want to go there with Tremaine. But today he didn't waste any time asking Trese for sex, and she didn't waste any time giving in. She didn't know if the blunt was creeping up on her, but she really wanted Tremaine; just as bad as he wanted her. He started kissing on her thighs making her feel more entwined in the moment. Trese rubbed Tremaine's head as she squirmed from the satisfaction that he was giving the lips between her thighs. He slowly pulled her boxers off so he could get more in tune without the interference of her clothes. He then gave her a more satisfying touch to the lips while she moaned from the pleasures of someone other than her man.

"Damn, Tremaine," Trese moaned with her eyes closed. Tremaine had that touch to caress Trese the way she craved for it. After he finished his oral pleasure on her, she returned the favor, and then they topped if off with rough intimate sex before the night was over.

Morning came and Vann still had not called Chanelle to arrange a meeting. Chanelle was beginning to wonder if Vann was going meet her. She decided to take the lead so she sent him a text message: *Great morning baby! Have you placed me in your schedule yet? Che'*

When Vann received the text message, he smiled but wondered why he had not heard from Trese. After getting ready for work, he checked his schedule to see when he could meet up with Chenelle.

He finally called her up. "Hey," Chenelle answered, with a smile spread from ear to ear. She was in her hotel room just about to leave for an early morning business meeting she had scheduled with one of her associates.

"So, ah what's up with ya?" Vann asked her.

"Not much, not much. Just about to head out to a meeting. What about you?" she asked him.

"I'm rolling to the work place now. Say, but ah, about us hooking up. It's gunna have to be Friday night. If that's cool with you?" Vann asked, yet directly told Chenelle.

"Oh, so Friday, huh?" she asked him for confirmation.

"Yeah, Friday. Is that cool?" he asked her again.

"Yes, it should be. I can't wait to see you. I've been thinking about you constantly. I mean, it's like crazy!" Chenelle told him.

"Girl, that's not crazy! It's just that we haven't seen each other in a while and don't trip because I've been thinking about you too ma," Vann told her with no hesitation.

"Oh, ok. I...," Chenelle was just about to agree with Vann but he completely cut her off.

"Well, I've made it up here to the job. Hit me up anytime you want, alright." Vann really did miss Chenelle and he wanted to make it clear that she wasn't the only one feeling the way she felt. After he hung up with her, he entered the building to grab some of his work before he left to go out on site.

After checking out one of the company trucks, he called Trese. Her phone went straight to voicemail. Vann was shocked because she usually did that when they were together.

"Hi, you've reached Tresey. I'm not available to take your call at this time. So leave me a reason to call you back." Beep.

"Oh so you forgot to call your boy huh...that's wassup. I'm not gunna trip with ya tho. Just hit me back when you

17

get this." Vann was a little upset talking to her voicemail. He didn't like having to leave *his* girl a message.

Trese was still sleep and Tremaine was right beside her. Usually she would call Vann right back; but this time she didn't. She usually talked to him before she went to work; but this time she didn't. She was slipping; laying up with Tremaine and not thinking about what Vann could possibly be doing. What if he had decided to surprise her that morning with a visit?

Trese then opened her eyes and, out of nowhere, she yelled at Tremaine, "Tremaine get your ass up!" She had forgotten that she was suppose to at least call Vann since she did tell him that she was going to work earlier than usual. But time had already passed and she was suppose to have been up before him. Trese was aggravated and scared. She wanted Tremaine to get up and get up fast so she could call Vann. Tremaine mumbled that he was getting up but he still didn't budge. He just turned on his other side. "Damn it Tre! Get up! I have to go to work!" Trese told him while pushing him off of the bed. Tremaine started to laugh as he got up off of the floor.

"Trese baby. You're tripping. You know I know that you have to go to work." Trese didn't say anything back to him. She just walked out and left Tremaine in the room by himself hoping that he would be gone when she came back.

She went to the bathroom to call Vann. When she turned her phone back on she noticed that she had a new voicemail. She had a feeling that it was from Vann so she didn't even bother checking it. She just scrolled to his name and called him.

Vann's phone rang but he didn't answer. Trese decided to call back. Not sounding too excited Vann answered the phone, "Wassup?"

"Hey baby!" Trese said. "I saw you called. Is something wrong?" she asked him.

"Nah I'm alright. But ah, let me holla at you in a minute. I'm busy," Vann was still a little upset.

"Okay," she said.

After Vann hung up the phone, he continued driving to his first property to inspect. Trese got ready for work all the while wondering why Vann sounded so far away with her, so distant. However, deep down inside, her conscience was getting to her because she knew she had slipped. Tremaine had already left while she was in the bathroom on the phone with Vann. After leaving her apartment, she called Peaches and told her that she was on her way to pick her up.

Circles

## 2. THE UNEXPECTED

FRIDAY MORNING, GREEDY was awakened by the two pits he had in his backyard. Greedy looked out his bedroom window trying to see why his dogs were barking.

"Damn! You didn't feed them this morning did you Gena?" Greedy asked his girl while he walked towards the bathroom.

Still lying down with her eyes closed, Gena answered, "Nah!" Greedy just shook his head and finished up in the bathroom. When he was done, he walked out of the bedroom and immediately saw Chase still asleep in the living room on the couch.

Greedy stayed in the South Dallas area. He was a young buck, 22 years old, who had nothing on his mind but making money. He was a hustler to the heart. Greedy was the one who ran the streets and trouble always had his name all over it.

He walked over to the couch where Chase was laying. Greedy slapped the back of the couch real hard and yelled,

"Chase wake yo ass up, nigga!"
Chase jumped up like he heard gunshots or something, "Say bro..." Chase looked at Greedy like he was a stranger off the street.

"What's up man?" Greedy shot back as he stepped back because it appeared as though Chase was ready to get a nigga. Greedy started laughing and just said, "Go feed those dogs for me bro."

"Aight my nigga! Next time just tap a nigga or something," Chase told him. Then Chase walked out to the back to feed the dogs and Greedy went back to his room.

"Gena! Why yo ass didn't feed my babies this morning?" he asked her as he shoved her on her side.

"What? Boy, stop," she said.

"Boy stop? Gena, do I look like a boy to you? Baby, I'm

20

a man and right now your man needs for you to cook him some breakfast. Now get yo ass up!" Greedy demanded while slapping her on the butt.

Gena then turned over and kissed Greedy on his lower back. "Baby, do I have to? I'm tired. You kept me up last night."

Greedy turned around and gave Gena a kiss on the lips. "Now can I get some breakfast?" he asked her.

"Well...," Gena said while still lying down.

"Man, get yo ass up. I have some business to take care of and I'm not about to keep telling yo ass either!" Greedy started to get a little irritated because Gena was playing a little bit too much. She finally got up after she saw that Greedy was getting upset.

Greedy's cell phone started ringing so he picked up and saw that it was Lace. Lace was this chick he once messed around with. She worked at a strip club in Ag Town (Arlington) called Hard Body's.

"What the fuck she want?" Greedy mumbled to himself as he answered his phone. "What's good, what's good?" Greedy asked her.

"Hey, did you get that for me?" Lace asked him.

"Get what?" he asked her.

"What you think? I need them for tonight. You still coming by right?" she asked him.

"By the strip...oh yeah I got that. You said four, right?" Greedy asked.

"Yeah, I did say four. But bring some more just in case. You know how shit be popping off at the strip," she said.

"Yeah that's a bet. Make sure you get ready for me too baby girl," Greedy told her.

Lace smiled, "Alright baby."

After hanging up with Lace, Greedy jumped in the shower while Gena was in the kitchen cooking breakfast. When Chase came back inside from feeding the dogs, he went right back to the couch and laid down.

Chase was Gena's little brother and Greedy's homeboy since high school. Chase was mixed with black and Hispanic; of course his mama was black and his daddy was Hispanic. His complexion was a dirty light brown. His eyes were dark brown and his hair was wavy, black, and short cut. He was a tall, slim version of the daddy which he really knew nothing about. All he really knew about family was that his big sister Gena had been there for him and her boyfriend Greedy was like the brother he never had. Greedy and Chase were real close; so close that they would do anything for one another at no matter the cost.

When she finished cooking, Gena fixed two plates and placed them on the table. "Baby, your breakfast is ready; and Chase I fixed you a plate too," Gena yelled while puffing on her black.

"Aight!" Greedy shouted as he stepped out of the shower. Gena didn't have to tell Chase twice; he hurried up and ran to the kitchen table.

Gena was standing by the kitchen sink when Greedy entered the kitchen. "You know Jewell and Tracie hit a clean lick on them checks last week and that nigga Keeno got half of that shit," Gena told Greedy. Greedy looked at her with a disgusted look on his face, clearly not too pleased to hear the words which came out of Gena's mouth. Tracie was Greedy's baby sister. She was eighteen and usually was the person Gena would go to for the checks and ID's.

"Oh, yeah…," Greedy said.

"Man your sister has a hoe ass nigga for a baby daddy; and Jewell's bitch ass...OOOOO! I can't stand that red bitch there!" Chase said while licking his fingers.

Greedy didn't waste any time talking. After they finished their breakfast, he and Chase went straight over to T-Baby's crib after breakfast. Tracie didn't stay too far from them; she stayed in East Dallas off Lagow. Greedy and Chase jumped in Greedy's 2005 Lexus. Chase rolled up a blunt while Greedy made a move towards his sister's crib. Greedy was upset because he knew his sister was smarter than that. Plus, he also knew how messy Gena's ass was.

Pulling up in front of Tracie's crib, Greedy and Chase peeped out the scenery. "It looks like T-Baby is still here; I don't see her BD tho," Chase said. Greedy really didn't care. He just wanted to see what was up with his baby sister.

Before Greedy walked up to the door, he tried to get in touch with Darren, but he didn't get an answer. So Greedy left a message telling Darren to call him back ASAP.

Darren was too busy at work. He planned on leaving earlier than usual and he had a lot to do before he left the office. He was taking the rest of the day off because it was Friday and he had some things to take care of.

Darren looked down at his phone and saw that the missed call showed Greedy's name. Darren thought to himself, *Man, what in the hell this nigga want?* He picked up the phone and got the alert that he had a new voice message. He listened to the message that was left by Greedy. After he heard the message, Darren decided that he wasn't going to call Greedy until after he left work. It wasn't too long before it was actually time for Darren to leave the workplace. Instead, he started wondering how things were going with his boy Vann; remembering that he had made plans with his ex-girl, Chenelle. So, he decided to call him to see what was up.

Vann was stretched across his bed when he felt his cell phone vibrating next to him. He picked it up, "Yeah."

"What's up bro!" Darren asked sounding like he was the one going on the date.

"Shit, ain't nothing right now. I'm still stretched out. What you got for me?" Vann asked him.

Darren started laughing, "Not a'mutha fucking thang! Did you talk to o'girl?"

"You talking about Chenelle bro?" Vann asked.

"Yeah," Darren said.

"Yeah. I told her that we could hook up today. I still need to talk to her and tell her what I have planned for her," Vann told Darren.

"Well do what you do playa. I was just hollering at ya," Darren told him.

"Aight bro," Vann said while hanging up.

After he hung up the phone, Vann turned over on his back and stared at the ceiling thinking about Chenelle...and then Trese. He was feeling sort of displaced with himself. Vann was missing Trese, but he knew he wanted to connect with Chenelle.

Before he met Trese, he and Chenelle had a little thing going on before she took her job offer in Houston. He was once wrapped up into Chenelle and she was wrapped up into him

# Circles

too. But, as soon as she dropped the bomb on him about moving from Dallas to Houston, he started to change. His actions started becoming more and more selfish and foolish. Chenelle was hurt by the way he treated her before she moved. When they went their separate ways, they were on bad terms. However, after some time had passed, Chenelle decided to call Vann just to see how he was doing. At that point, they made short lived amends. As time continued to progress, they slowly drifted apart and that's when Vann met Trese. Eventually, Vann changed his number when the relationship between him and Trese began to get serious. When Chenelle tried to call him later on, there was a message saying that his phone was out of service. So, Chenelle didn't really get upset because she knew, deep down inside, that they were too far apart to try and maintain a relationship. As an alternative, she just occupied her time with work; that's until she met Gerald, also known as Greedy.

Greedy was from the South, but not from the Houston area. This brother was in Houston taking care of some major business running some check hustles with his sister Tracie. They had been running check licks since Greedy finished high school. Keeno and Six, Tracie's baby daddy and his homeboy, introduced Greedy to the game. It was a group of them in Houston for that week. They would travel every two or three weeks and hit check licks in different states and in different spots. It was Greedy, Tracie, Six, and Keeno this round and the checks were running smoothly.

While walking through Wal-Mart, Greedy peeped game when he saw Chenelle in the Personal Hygiene aisle. Chenelle noticed that she was being admired by Greedy so she turned and glanced back at him. He smiled and was like damn. Greedy was a nice looking guy himself. He was clean cut, 5'9, thick but nice in size, muscular chest and arms, and didn't have any permanent gold in his mouth, but was wearing his grill at the time. Chenelle smiled back. At first, she was really not trying to flirt; just being polite. But Greedy didn't waste any more time as he made his way towards her while she was standing by her basket. He rubbed his chin and looked Chenelle up and down. He couldn't believe this girl was looking this damn fine and was standing in front of him. Greedy had on his white tee with his starched monkey jeans and his all white Forces. Chenelle was looking classy as usual. She had on her fitted bebe jeans, a bebe blouse, and she was rocking her bebe heels with her 14k princess cut diamond earrings. Her nails were done and her hair was in a wrap nicely trimmed with honey highlights.

"Um!" Greedy was just about to compliment her when she flipped it on him. "Um...um what? You like what you see?" Chenelle asked him.

"Of course I do, or I wouldn't have tried to approach you. I mean before I was rudely interrupted, I was just about to tell you that your money was hanging out of your purse," he replied with a very condescending attitude.

Chenelle then looked down at her purse and saw her money hanging out. She looked back up and smiled, "Why thank you. What is your name?" she asked.

"Gerald. And what's yours ma?" he asked her.

"Chenelle," she told him with no hesitation.

"I noticed that you talk like you're not from here," he mentioned.

"Oh, I'm not. I just moved here about a year ago for school and a job offer," she replied.

"So, where you from?" Greedy asked her.

"I'm from Dallas. And you?" she asked him.

"I'm from South Dallas. You know where the action is?" he asked.

"Where the action is, I guess," she offered with a sly smile.

"You guess what? What part are you from? Wait a minute, I bet you're from the Cliff right?" he asked.

"Yes and what's wrong with the Cliff?" she asked him.

"Ain't nothing mama. Ain't nothing with it. So, did you live in the hood?" Greedy asked.

"The hood! What's wrong with the hood? You think I'm a hood rat or something?" Chenelle asked him. She was getting a little upset and started to walk away.

Greedy grabbed her hand, "Hold on mama. I didn't mean to offend you....okay before you walk away from me can I at least call you sometime?"

Chenelle stopped and turned around and looked at

25

# Circles

Greedy for a moment. She thought he was very good looking, she was very attracted to him, and most, he looked like he had some money. "You can call me," she gave in.

"Oh yeah," he asked with a surprising smile. Chenelle and Greedy exchanged numbers. After they parted, Chenelle checked out of the store and left while Greedy went over to customer service to make his return for some cash.

While he was standing in line, his cell phone rang. He looked at it and saw that it was his sister. "What's taking you so long? Are you ok?" Tracie asked him.

"Yeah, I'll be out in a minute," he snapped at her.

"Alright, you need to speed it up a little," she demanded.

Greedy made his way back to the car and they left to go work two more Wal-Mart stores. Afterwards, they went back to the hotel where Six was still hanging around. He didn't go with them for that round because he was going to go the next day.

Greedy and Chenelle hooked up before he left to go back to Dallas. She couldn't believe the time that was spent between them. What they shared was exactly what she really needed and wanted. Greedy was just the man to give it to her. Everything was all good with Greedy and Chenelle until after he left. Greedy and his crew stayed in Houston for about two weeks and he had to go back home after the work they had to do was finished. Chenelle wasn't upset because she knew what type of work Greedy was doing. But, there was one thing bothering her, the loss of his sex. She and Greedy had mad sex but the last time they had sex it was unprotected. So she was a little nervous, thinking she might have gotten pregnant. Chenelle wasn't for sure, so she made an appointment at the local clinic. She spoke to Greedy and told him about her concern so he would be well aware if the unthinkable was to have gone down.

"Finally," Chenelle sighed softly to herself as she pulled up to the clinic. While sitting inside the clinic's parking lot, she took a deep breath and then got out of her car and walked into the clinic. She felt as if all eyes were on her when in actuality no one was even paying any attention to her. She signed in, took a seat, and waited for her name to be called.

It wasn't too long before the nurse called Chenelle to go back for her exam. She took a pregnancy test, which came back negative. Chenelle was so relieved. She figured that while she was there, she might as well go ahead and have her annual done too. Her results would not be back for a few days. Other than the tests that had to be sent off, the doctor told her that everything looked great and that the nurse would call to give her the rest of the results in three days.

Chenelle was cool with that and couldn't wait to tell Greedy the good news about her not being pregnant. It was great news to her because she knew that she couldn't handle a child right now. She thought to herself the sex was good but having a baby wasn't. She rushed to call him but he didn't answer. She wasn't big on leaving messages so she just decided to call him back a little later.

ON THE SECOND, the nurse from the clinic tried to contact Chenelle. She didn't get an answer so she left a message telling her to call the clinic ASAP. Chenelle didn't hear her phone ring because she was in her office trying to finish up some reports. She was expecting Greedy to call her since she hadn't heard from him so she jumped to the phone when she heard the message beep. She looked at her phone and saw that she had a new voice message. She became overwhelmed with relief because she just knew it was from Greedy. When she checked her voicemail, her relief turned to anxiety when she heard that Greedy was not the one who had left her a message. She was disappointed to hear the nurse's voice on the phone. Without listening to the entire message she hung up the phone quickly. Chenelle placed her hands over her face and started to cry. She figured Greedy had left her completely alone and didn't want anything to do with her because she had not heard from him in a while and she had left him message after message, and he never returned any of her calls.

In the midst of her tears, there was a knock at her office door. It was Dana, her colleague. Chenelle hurried up and wiped her tears with some Kleenex. But, she couldn't really hide it because Dana had already entered her office. "What's wrong, chica?" Dana asked.

"Nothing," Chenelle answered.

"Yes there is, and you're going to tell me," Dana said forcefully while pulling a chair up next to Chenelle.

# Circles

"Really its nothing. I'm just going through a lot right now. Just a little emotional, that's all, you know," Chenelle lied. She put her head down on her desk.

"Damn girl, something or someone is bugging the hell out of you. All I can say is cry until you can't cry anymore. Let the frustration and anger out that way, instead of doing something real stupid, okay," Dana tried to give her some woman to woman advice.

"Alright, girl. Thanks for the advice," Chenelle thankfully told her. Dana gave Chenelle a big hug and then left her to be alone. Chenelle closed and locked the door and then walked back to her desk. She finished up the work that she had to complete and then she left the office and headed towards her place.

On her way home, she thought about how she was living her life and why she always ended up heartbroken. She couldn't answer that question though.

As soon as she made it home, she replayed the message from earlier. "Hi, Chenelle. This is nurse Lippott and I have your test results back. If you would please call me back at 713-555-5555, I can give those results to you. Please call as soon as you can. Thanks." Chenelle listened to the message two more times wondering if the nurse had good news or bad. It was too late to call back so she had to wait and call the next day.

Chenelle had a hard time sleeping that night. She tossed and turned and she even woke up in cold sweats. She really was disturbed and frustrated.

Finally morning came and Chenelle was so tired from not getting any sleep through the night that she overslept. She was supposed to be at school at 9:00 a.m. and at work at noon, and it was already 11:17 a.m. She hurried and called the office to let her boss know that she was going to be a little late coming in. After she hung up with her boss, she called nurse Lippott back.

"Hi, this is Nurse Lippott," Nurse Lippott answered.

"Oh, hi! This is Chenelle Jones. You called and left me a message about my results," Chenelle reply nervously.

"Oh, yes, yes. Hold on for a minute while I get your file okay," she said.

"Okay."

# Heather Jornay Perkins

After keeping Chenelle on hold for about two minutes, she finally came back to the line, "Okay, Chenelle. I have your file. Let me see what your results are. Oh, you're positive on your results. So I will need for you to come in. You and your partner need observation and treatment."

"Positive? Positive for what? I was told that my pregnancy test came back negative," Chenelle shouted in frustration.

"No honey. You're positive for HIV," Nurse Lippott offered with sympathy in her voice.

"I'm positive....I'm positive for HIV," Chenelle said in a low tone. She paused after hearing that she had HIV; she held the phone in silence. The nurse allowed the moment of silence before she interjected to get Chenelle's attention. She repeated her request for Chenelle and her partner to come in to start the treatment process. Without hesitation, Chenelle agreed to come in.

After Chenelle hung up the phone, she felt a sick twisted feeling in her stomach. Her heart was feeling an emotion of hurt and she fell to the floor in a waterfall of tears. She started throwing things and yelling about how she couldn't believe what Gerald had done to her. She prayed and prayed. She had never experienced this type of feeling ever before. She started to feel helpless, hopeless, worthless, trapped, and like it was the end for her. Then she started to think about Gerald and why she was now a victim of HIV. She wanted to call him, but she didn't because she was still very disturbed by the fact she had HIV and that he was the one who gave it to her. So she made the decision not to call him. Chenelle wanted to confront him in person instead of telling him over the phone.

A few hours had passed before Chenelle pulled herself together and went to work. As soon as she made it in, she told her boss that she needed some time off and that she was going to use her vacation time. Her boss agreed to let her off but she still needed to complete some work that was already assigned to her. He gave her as much time as she needed. Chenelle was glad that her boss agreed to let her off just in enough time to go and pack and head to Dallas.

Before she left she went to the clinic and the doctor explained everything to her that she needed to know about the

## Circles

disease and what treatments were provided. He gave her
a prescription and she went to the pharmacy and got it filled.
After everything that she was exposed to, she was still in a
major state of shock. She could not understand how she could
have been so stupid to have unprotected sex with Gerald.
Chenelle gathered her things and left heading towards Dallas.
And that's when she found herself in front of Vann's apartment
with a note, taping it to his front door.

Heather Jornay Perkins

Circles

## 3. LIKE OLD TIMES

AS FRIDAY BEGAN to unfold, Vann and Chenelle had
planned to meet up later on that evening. Before the evening
took place Vann ran a couple of errands. He went to Knock
Outs to get a hair cut, to the bank, and then he made
reservations for The Craft at the W Hotel, which was Chenelle's
favorite restaurant in Dallas.

Vann couldn't wait to see Chenelle; however his mind
was steadily drifting away thinking about Trese. By hurting
Trese, it really didn't do anything but hurt him too. He still
wasn't going to call her until after he spent his time with
Chenelle. He wanted to give Trese enough time to cool down a
bit.

After he made the reservations, it seemed as though
time was just ticking away and, before he knew it, it was going
on 4 o'clock. He realized that he hadn't even called Chenelle
to confirm. Just as he was about to call Chenelle, Trese called
him. Vann looked at his cell phone and was surprised to see
that it was Trese calling him back so quickly. He didn't answer
because he knew if he did Trese would want to make up and
that was not the plan. Vann had other things on his agenda
that he needed to take care of before him and his girl made up.

After his phone stopped ringing, he hurried up and
called Chenelle. The phone rang a couple of times before
Chenelle finally picked it up. Chenelle was at the nail shop
getting a fill on her nails. "Hey, wassup, Vann!" she said.

"You," he told her. Chenelle had such a big smile on
her face, that she actually started to blush.

"So, what are we getting into? Have you made up your
mind yet?" she asked him.

"A little bit of everything, I have something
planned for ya. Just make sure you look good for ya boy," he
lightheartedly told her.

"Okay, I'll make sure of that," she answered back obediently.

"So, just meet me at my place around 7:30 p.m., and be on time too Chenelle," Vann demanded. He knew that Chenelle was notorious for being late at times.

"Don't worry I will be there on time," she assured him.

Chenelle hung up with Vann and continued to get her nails filled. While she was relaxing at the nail shop, she thought about her situation and what kind of mess she was in. Her plan was to eventually get around to seeing Greedy and tell him what was really going on. She knew that she owed him that much because he needed to get checked out himself and whomever else he had come in contact with unprotected.

Chenelle sat there and continued to ponder on how she was going to break the news to Greedy. Not even knowing where he was brought about the most confusion for her. How was she going to get to him, she thought. What Chenelle didn't know was that Greedy was not far from where she was. He was over at his sister's place trying to see what happened to the loot. It was really none of his business but Greedy intended on knowing because he was that kind of person; nosey.

There were kids playing out front in Tracie's front yard. Greedy and Chase finally got out the car and walked up and his niece approached him. "Hey Unc!" his niece shouted while holding her hand out for some money.

"Hey, baby girl. Now why is it that every time I come over here you gotta hit me up for some money?" Greedy asked his niece.

"Because I'm broke!" she told him. Greedy and Chase started laughing and then Greedy gave his niece five dollars and then they went on inside.

As soon as they walked in, Tracie was a little surprised to see Greedy. "Hey! What are you doing here?" Tracie was standing in her hallway.

"I can't come and see my baby sister?" he asked while grinning and reaching over to give her a big hug.

"What's up T-Baby!" Chase said.

"Hey Chase," she spoke back. After hugging her brother, Tracie went back to her room and Greedy followed right behind her.

# Circles

"Where's Jewell's red ass at?" Greedy asked his sister.

"Oh, she went over to Shante's to get her hair done," Tracie told him.

"So what's up with this Keeno shit?" Greedy asked her.

"What Keeno shit?" Tracie repeated the question trying to be a smart ass.

"You know with the money issue. I know you just not giving this nigga money like that, after the shit he pulled with you last time!" Greedy stated sternly.

"Man! I gave that boy what he needed for his lawyer," Tracie said.

"Yeah, that's what he said huh? Baby sis, don't let that nigga run game on you like that," Greedy told her. Greedy was beginning to get even more upset than he was before he left to go see his sister. He stepped out of the room leaving the conversation at that. Greedy went into the kitchen and poured himself a glass of water. After he sipped his water he and Chase left.

Greedy was still trying to get in contact with Darren. Darren was finally on his way out when he received a call from his baby mama, Sonya.

"Yeah, what's good with ya?" he asked.

"I thought you were coming by?" Sonya asked. She was a little upset with Darren because he was supposed to have come by last Sunday. A week had passed and Darren was supposed to be spending time with his son Daron.

Sonya and Darren met three years ago and had their son, Daron along the way. Darren was a good father. It was just that he had been extremely busy with work lately and Sonya was the type who wanted to go out and bullshit all the time. He hadn't forgotten that he was supposed to be spending time with his little boy. So he told Sonya that he would come and pick him up this weekend.

After hanging up with her, he called Greedy back to see what was up with him. "What's up son?" Darren said.

"Yeah, nigga! I've been trying to get at you all fucking day!" Greedy told him.

"Nigga! You knew I was at work, wassup?" Darren asked.

"Yeah, those niggas in Bertrand got that good. You

34

hear me? Shit, we need to check it out and see where they getting that good from cause we ain't trying to lose. Shit we in it fo' real. It's a fool my nigga, it's a fool!" Greedy told him.

"Oh yeah...I'll see what I can do on my end aight," Darren told him.

"Fa sho, you got it," Greedy said. Greedy hung up with Darren and then called Vann.

It was going on 6:50 p.m. and Vann was finally back at his place. He saw that he had two voice messages and five missed calls on his phone. The first voicemail was from his boy, Greedy, "Wassup, nigga? This ya boy Gerald aka Greedy. Get back at me cause it's ah fool my nigga fo' real!"

The second voicemail was from his mother, "Hey baby, this is your mother. I haven't heard from you in a couple of weeks. Is everything ok? Love you."

He then looked at his missed calls and saw that Trese was really the person who was trying to reach him as the rest of the missed calls were from her. *That girl is tripping! I'm not calling her back; at least not tonight,* Vann thought to himself. Vann had everything planned out for Chenelle. With just the two of them and no interruptions, the night was going to be the best.

Vann looked at the time and saw how fast the time was going by and he was nowhere near ready. He remembered telling Chenelle to be at his place at 7:30, so he hurried and picked out something to wear. He picked out his starched down Mecca jeans, his brown, white, and cream Mecca shirt, and his all white Air Force Ones. If there wasn't anything else Vann could put together, he could hook up his wardrobe. After laying out his clothes, he took a quick shower, and then finished getting himself ready for Chenelle.

On the other side of town, Chenelle was getting ready herself. She was almost ready and just about to walk out of the door. Chenelle had on her Baby Phat blue jean pants outfit, with some nice blue jean heels she had bought from Baker's. Her hair was in a ponytail with the Chinese bangs. Chenelle was looking good for the night and she knew Vann wouldn't be disappointed. She took one last glance at herself in the mirror and smacked her lips together keeping her nude lipstick moist. After glancing at herself, she then grabbed her Baby Phat blue

# Circles

jean purse and her keys and headed out the door. While driving towards Vann's crib, she called him to let him know that she was on her way.

Vann was finally ready. He threw on some Nautica cologne, because he remembered how Chenelle use to like him wearing it. He couldn't wait to see Chenelle. He made sure his place was nice and clean and smelling fresh. The night was going so well that it was like it was meant for Vann and Chenelle to reconnect.

While Vann was having a moment, there was a knock at the door. "Hold on!" Vann yelled from his bedroom. He turned the lights off in his bedroom and then walked towards the door. While taking deep breaths, he opened the door. Vann was amazed as he thought Chenelle looked stunning. Chenelle was smiling so hard that she started laughing. She came in and gave Vann a huge hug. She couldn't believe that she was finally hugging him. She was so happy to see him after being away from him for so long without any contact.

"Hey baby!" Chenelle hopped into Vann's arms and held him very closely and tightly. Vann knew that she had missed him and he couldn't do anything but laugh and hug her back.

"Wassup girl, I missed you too." Chenelle hopped down and Vann closed the door behind her. "Damn girl, you're looking good. I guess yo nigga treating you good, huh?" Vann asked her.

"Is he…because I didn't think so. But, I do know who can," Chenelle said while kissing Vann on his neck. Chenelle didn't hide the fact that she wanted Vann really bad. She really didn't care what anyone said; all she wanted was Vann.

"Girl, you better stop before you get yourself in a whole lot of something you can't get yourself out of," Vann told her while grabbing her hands.

"Why?" Chenelle asked him.

"Okay, look. I have something planned for you tonight and let's just roll with it alright." Vann told her,

"Okay, whatever," Chenelle said. Chenelle sat down on the couch and Vann sat right beside her. He slightly touched her face and then leaned over and kissed her very softly and passionately. He knew he told her not to go there but he wanted her just as bad as she wanted him. The temptation between them was very alluring and the moment that they were having was one to cherish. Old feelings started to come back for Chenelle. Although she kept her situation in the forefront of her mind, she really wanted Vann. But what can you expect; after all Vann was her first love. She couldn't resist the touch of Vann because she wanted Vann to make her feel like a woman should. "Umm, that was nice," she said in a moan. Vann smiled, got up, picked up his keys, and then they both headed out of the door.

Vann drove his car instead of letting Chenelle drive hers. On the way to the restaurant, he put on some R. Kelly to set the mood. Chenelle didn't bother talking to Vann during the ride downtown; they just road and enjoyed the sultry tunes of Robert all the way there.

It was 8:01 p.m. by the time Vann pulled up to the valet in front of the hotel. After they entered the restaurant and were seated, they started catching up with each other a bit. "So, what have you been doing since you've been back in town?" Vann asked her.

"Well, nothing really. I've been working and trying to figure out some things. And I still haven't gone over to my parents house," she explained.

"What are you trying to figure out mami?" he asked her.

"It's nothing to be discussing right now," she replied praying that that conversation would disappear. The waitress came over and took their order. As the time past, Vann and Chenelle enjoyed their dinner and time reminiscing on their past relationship together.

After having a nice time at The Craft and getting drunk, Vann and Chenelle went back to her hotel room. As soon as they made it through the door, Chenelle threw her purse and heels on the floor and trampled to the bathroom with Vann right behind her. He was trying to act as though he wasn't feeling the drinks, but he was.

WHILE MAINTAINING HIS composure, he sat on her bed and made himself comfortable. Chenelle then came out of the bathroom and sat beside him. She spun her ponytail up into a

# Circles

ball and then asked Vann if he cared for something else to drink. Vann told her no because he knew he couldn't take another sip of anything or he would be out for the count. Vann really didn't want the night to go by without trying to make a move on her. So he leaned towards Chenelle and kissed her lips softly. Chenelle sighed with a moan, letting Vann know that she wanted every bit that he wanted to give her. They started to kiss each other aggressively and the passion between them was so amazing that they became overly anxious to have one another. Vann laid her down and continued to kiss and rub on her body as Chenelle politely accepted his touch. She wanted him so badly, but all she could think about was what she had contracted from Greedy and how it would affect Vann if he knew about it. But Chenelle didn't stop Vann. She couldn't resist him and her hormones took control and told her that all she wanted was to have sex with him. However, she was at least considerate enough to not allow him to enter her bare. She made sure she gave him protection to use with her. Deep down inside, she knew that she should have told him but she also knew that it wouldn't have gone as far as it did.

After their passionate night of great sex, Vann woke up to an early morning phone call from Trese. He looked at his phone and just pressed decline because he wasn't in the mood to talk to Trese. Besides, he had Chenelle lying right beside him. Vann turned his cell phone off because he knew how Trese was and that she would have just kept calling. His phone was right next to the bed and on the floor he saw a magnum condom wrapper that had never been opened. *Damn! I know I didn't do that shit*, he thought to himself. He turned on his back and then took a deep breath. Vann wanted to wake Chenelle up and ask her if they used one because he was so messed up that he couldn't really remember. So, he turned around and wrapped his arms around her and kissed her softly on her neck.

"Umm, baby your lips are so soft, did you know that?" Chenelle asked him while inhaling his cologne scent. Vann didn't say anything. He just smiled and kissed her again. "So, I guess you already know, huh?" she asked him.

"Yeah, that's what they say. Say Chenelle did we use a condom last night?" Vann asked her.

"What! You don't remember?" she asked him.

"Hell nah. I was too messed up," he told her while looking doubtful and confused.

"Baby, of course. I told you I didn't want to go bare and that's when you pulled out two or three condoms out of your pocket. So yep we did. Why do you ask?" she asked him with concern.

"Shit because I knew I was messed up and I really didn't remember. But, I do remember one thing," he said.

"What?" she asked.

"You were moaning my name," Vann said while laughing.

"Boy, that's not funny!" Chenelle said enjoying his humor.

Vann finally got out the bed and then he looked at his watch for the time. It was 9:28 a.m. He put his clothes back on and then leaned over to kiss Chenelle while she was still in the bed wrapped up in the covers. Chenelle really didn't want him to leave so she gave him that OH HELL TO THE NO!!! look and he just grinned and told her that he would stay in touch. Chenelle didn't chase after him because she didn't want to look too desperate. She turned around towards the coffee table by her bed and she picked up a chocolate covered strawberry and poured a glass of Blackberry wine. Chenelle knew that it was too early for that but her nerves were working her that morning.

While Vann was on his way to his crib, he checked his voicemail and, what do you know, Trese left a message,

"Baby, please call me I need to talk to you. It's important."

When Vann finally made it to his place he gave Trese a call, "Wassup?"

"What do you mean wassup? I've been calling and calling and you can't even pick up the damn phone!" Trese was highly pissed at Vann. She was frustrated and upset with Vann.

"Man, Trese. I didn't call you to argue. Wassup shit you called me and said it was important. So what's so important?" Vann asked her.

"We are. Me and you, that's what! You've been acting all shady. Wassup with that?" she asked him.

# Circles

"I'm not acting shady with you. I was just giving you sometime to yourself; and allowing you to blow off some steam and shit. But it looks like you're still in that mood and you need a little more time," Vann said. Trese frowned and her emotions took over her as she was more sad than mad. She didn't say anything back to Vann she just hung up the phone. Vann didn't care why she had hung up because he wasn't in his right mind to be calling her back anyway. Trese was so angry and hurt by Vann's actions towards her. She didn't waste anytime by showing up at Vann's crib unannounced. It took her a minute to get there.

Vann was just getting out of the shower when he heard a knock at the door. He didn't quickly respond to the knock. He crept to the door and then looked out the peephole. "Damn!" he said softly. It was Trese at his door and she didn't look too happy either. Vann didn't hesitate; he just opened the door and Trese rushed in crying.

"Why do you have to treat me like this Vann?" Vann calmly closed the door and then took Trese by the hand and pulled her close to him. Vann had his towel wrapped around his waist and he was still wet from the shower. Trese was still crying and Vann really couldn't stand for his girl to cry. He embraced her with a hug. Holding her tightly, he apologized for hurting her feelings.

"I'm sorry baby. You just be coming at me in the wrong way. You know I can't stand being away from you and I know you can't stand being away from me. But, you have to understand that we are not perfect boo and there are things we do that have no meanings to be explained," Vann told her as he wiped her tears away from her cheeks. She smiled a little and then Vann turned around, locked his door, and then he took Trese to his bedroom. All Vann wanted to do was lay down and get some major rest. After the night with Chenelle, he was worn out. So all he did was lay down with Trese while still in his towel. He held her closely giving her the comfort she needed.

Heather Jornay Perkins

Circles

## 4. THE BREAKING NEWS

WHILE VANN AND Trese were cuddling back at his place, time was moving expeditiously for Chenelle. She was in search for Greedy; she needed to contact him as soon as possible. Chenelle remembered him saying something about him being from South Dallas so that's where she started. Chenelle had a home-girl that she knew from school, named of Jewell, who was from South Dallas and she figured she would be the best person to lead her to Greedy. What Chenelle wasn't aware of was that Jewell was not only her friend from school, but she was also a business partner of Greedy's and a running mate of his sister Tracie. They all ran the check business together.

Chenelle pulled up on Colonial Street right in front of Jewell's grandmother's house. No one was standing outside, like they usually are, so she parked and walked up to Jewell's grandmother's front door. She knocked on the door, but no one answered. Chenelle began to panic until she remembered that she had Jewell's cell phone number stored in her phone. She went to her address book, scrolled down until she reached Jewell's number, and called her up. Luckily, Jewell still had the same number. "Wassup, who is this?" Jewell answered.

"Hey girl! This Che'!" Chenelle said sounding excited.

"Girl wassup?! Where you been hiding?" Jewell asked her.

"Girl you know I moved to Houston and lately I've just been trying to get my shit together."

"Oh okay. Where are you now?" Jewell asked her.

"Just left your granny's house looking for you. Where are you?" Chenelle inquired.

"Oh, I'm over my best friend's brother's crib. We just chilling, kicking it, and shit like that. Come over here. I'm just around the corner," Jewell told her.

"Oh, okay, that's wassup," Chenelle said while putting

her car into drive. Jewell stayed on the phone and gave her directions.

Chenelle made it there in no time. She approached the front door not knowing what to expect. When she knocked, Jewell immediately answered the door. "Hey girl!" Jewell said after she opened the door for Chenelle. They both hugged. "Girl, I already told everyone that my girl Che' was on her way, so everyone this is Che' and Che' this is everyone."

After Jewel introduced Chenelle to everyone, she walked over and got her a drink. Jewell was at Greedy's place and everyone who usually kicked it with them was there: Jewell, Tracie, Greedy, Gena, Darren, and Chase. Greedy was in the corner drinking and playing dominoes with Darren and Chase. When Greedy looked up to see that Che' was really Chenelle he didn't look too thrilled. After he made eye contact with her she smiled at him and Greedy slowly put his head back down and stared at his dominoes. Chenelle didn't approach him like she wanted to because she didn't know if he was involved with someone there or not. She just played it off and told Jewell that she had to step outside for a second to take an important call.

Chenelle stepped out on the front porch and went into a panic of shock when it hit her that she actually didn't have to go searching for Greedy like she thought she would. She couldn't believe that she ran into Greedy so quickly.

Greedy saw Chenelle leave out so he played it cool and pretended as though he was going to check out something in the back; however, his intensions were to get to Chenelle as quickly as he could. Greedy walked around to the front and that's when he saw Chenelle leaning up against the wooden pole. When she turned around, Greedy was standing there and all she could do was give him a big hug. "Damn! Girl you sho'll do know how to find ah nigga!" Greedy told her.

Chenelle laughed, "You're right. I was looking for you. Greedy you never returned my calls. I mean ever since I mentioned that I could be pregnant, it was like you didn't want anything to do with me." Greedy put his head down with the slickest grin on his face as if the situation was funny to him. Chenelle then took a deep breath. Just as she was about to tell him, he interrupted her by apologizing to her.

"Man, Chenelle I didn't mean to throw you off like that.

43

# Circles

But I'm with someone. I didn't want to just tell you because I really do cut for you. So are you pregnant?" he asked her. Chenelle was filled up with so much animosity that she couldn't even talk to him the way she wanted.

"Pregnant…pregnant, that ain't even why I came looking for you. I'm not pregnant; but there is something else, *Gerald*," she snapped at him with evil in her eyes and tone.

"What shit?" he asked her with an attitude.

"Do you really want to know, *Gerald*, do you?" Chenelle asked him with even more anger in her voice this time.

"Yeah and I'm glad you're not pregnant! I just want to know what else could there be bothering you?" Greedy asked her.

"Well, I went to the clinic and did the whole annual thing and I took all my tests, you know for STD's and stuff. And…," Chenelle started to cry silently. She placed her hands over her face, "Gerald I have HIV, and I got it from you," she said with melancholy, low tone.

"You say what?" Greedy frowned and was looking like are you fucking serious. Chenelle didn't respond. She just ran back to her car and then drove off. Greedy stood there in silence and shock. Then his silence and shock began to transform into anger. He couldn't believe what Chenelle just told him.

After Chenelle drove off, Greedy went back inside and slammed the back door almost breaking the glass. He threw his beer down on the kitchen floor and then paced back and forth in the hallway. Gena and everyone else heard the loud noises that Greedy was making. Gena looked down the hall and saw Greedy pacing back and forth like something was wrong. She walked over to him and asked was something bothering him. But he didn't answer. He just kept pacing back and forth. So Gena didn't stop asking him. She demanded an answer. Meanwhile, everyone had stopped what they were doing and all eyes were on Greedy.

After about the fourth time she asked him, Greedy grabbed her by her throat and threw her up against the wall, "Bitch, you know what the fuck is wrong with me! You know what the fuck is wrong! OOOOO!" Greedy was furious. Darren jumped up and ran to get Greedy off of Gena. Gena was crying, coughing, screaming, and rubbing her throat all while she was gasping for air.

"Calm down little nigga! Calm tha fuck down!" Darren told him while holding him back. Darren tried to calm Greedy down but it was like he was powerless compared to him at this point. Everyone was screaming and shouting, overwhelmed by Greedy's actions. Greedy was not being himself and he knew it. But all he could think about was what Chenelle told him.

After Darren was finally able to get him off of Gena, Greedy went into his room and threw every piece of clothing out of his drawers. He was now looking for his pistol. Greedy was feeling so displaced after learning that someone had given him HIV; and he still had questions about who had given it to him.

He finally found his pistol under his mattress. Greedy had the pistol gripped tightly and was headed towards the living room, when Darren blocked the doorway. Gena was in the living room with Jewell on the couch. Tracie was standing by the doorway with Darren. Chase was in the room with Greedy trying to calm him down and get the pistol away from him. Greedy overlooked Chase and tried to walk out the bedroom but Darren was still blocking the doorway.

"Man, you are tripping right now fool! Let us know what is up! Shit, nigga! You pulling out guns and shit! Let us know what tha fuck is going on G?" Darren was getting angry himself. Greedy was still trying to pass Darren with his pistol still gripped tightly in his left hand. Everyone started asking questions after questions causing him to get even more entangled with fury. So Greedy fired his pistol up in the air putting a hole in the ceiling."

"Ya'll want to know what tha fuck is wrong with me? Ask that bitch on the couch, huh! Ask her how she fucked me up!" Greedy shouted. He shouted loud enough to where Gena could hear him.

"What tha fuck did I do to you Greedy? What did I do?" Gena stood up from the couch yelling back at him while storming towards their bedroom. Jewell hurried and grabbed her. Darren immediately told Jewell to take Gena away from the house.

45

# Circles

Greedy really wanted to hurt Gena and the bad part was that no one really knew why. No one else knew the pain that was finally erupting in his stomach. Greedy suddenly had tears rolling down his face. No one had ever seen him like this. "Darren this girl did me dirty fool! OOOOO! I just want to kill that hoe, ya hear me!"

Darren slowly approached Greedy trying to get closer and closer to him to get in reach of the pistol. He slowly took the pistol away from him and handed it to Chase. Chase then took the pistol and put it in the garage and placed it in a safe spot where no one could find it. Darren pulled Greedy towards him and hugged him tightly, "It's going to be alright bro, it's going to be alright."

Tracie was still on the side of the doorway and she was so stunned that she didn't know what to say. Greedy was her brother and she didn't know what was really bothering him; but she knew it had to be something serious. Greedy didn't want to talk to anyone, but Darren. Darren was the only one who could reach out to him at that time. So Tracie left and went back to her place.

Tracie drove all the way home with a knot in her throat trying not to cry from the thought of seeing her brother hurt so badly. When she pulled up, she saw that her baby daddy Keeno was there along with Jewell and Gena. As soon as Tracie walked through the door, Keeno couldn't wait to hear what the deal was with her brother. "Damn, T-Baby! What's up with your brother?" Keeno asked.

"I don't know! He won't talk to anyone but his boys. Whatever it is, it's between him and Gena. I've never seen him so hurt," she told him while visibly sharing her brother's pain. Gena was so hurt that she continued to cry and cry while sitting at the kitchen table with Jewell sitting across from her.

"You should've seen that nigga Keeno. He was actually trying to kill this girl," Jewell told him.

"Damn! That's fucked up! Why is that nigga so mad and shit?" Keeno asked. Tracie couldn't say; really no one could. All they knew was that he was saying Gena messed him up.

"Gena do you know what my brother was accusing you of?" Tracie asked.

"No I don't and it doesn't make any sense because all I ever did for him was love him and keep him happy," she responded while still sobbing in tears. Gena was even more so upset and sad about the fact that she couldn't put together what was bothering Greedy and what he was blaming her for.

Back at her hotel, Chenelle was so upset after she left that she almost wrecked herself out on the way back to her hotel room. As soon as she made it to her room, she placed a DO NOT DISTURB sign on her door. She couldn't believe that she finally told Greedy the truth and she was relieved that she did because it was tearing her up inside.

She really needed someone to talk to so she tried calling Dana her co-worker. Dana's voicemail picked up so Chenelle left her a message telling her that she really needed to talk to her. After leaving Dana a message Chenelle laid down on the bed and fell asleep. After all of the crying and all of the emotions that were built up from telling Greedy, she was drained.

Back at Greedy's crib, Darren, Chase, and Greedy all sat down at the kitchen table and Greedy was about to drop the bomb. But, he really didn't want to just jump right in and tell them without Vann being there too. He only wanted to say it one time. So Darren hit Vann up.

Vann and Trese were still laying next to one another. He couldn't hear his phone because he had it set to vibrate. But, luckily, he felt it. He reached over, looked at the caller id, and saw that it was Darren. He picked up, "Yeah what's good?" Vann asked while clearing his throat.

"Say, come over to Greedy's crib. Some shit just went down and Greedy asked for you to come my nigga. This is some real shit. Real talk," Darren told him.

"Aight bro. I'm on my way," Vann said. Vann hurried and threw something on real quick.

"Baby, where are you going?" Trese asked him.

"Man, this nigga Greedy got himself into some shit and I have to go and see what's up," he responded.

"Oh for real. Dang," she replied while still lying down.

"Baby, you gunna be aight tho right? I'ma ah head over here and if you leave just lock up and leave my key up under the mat, alright," Vann said while kissing her on the forehead.

# Circles

He then quickly left and headed over to Greedy's place.

Vann made it over there in no time. Before he pulled up, Greedy, Chase, and Darren had already smoked about two blunts and was working on the third one. Greedy was in there rapping and getting krunk trying to blow off some steam… the usual. So, when Vann arrived at the front door, he thought everything was cool because he heard his boy rapping his ass off. The guys didn't hear Vann knocking, so he just walked in. As soon as he did, Greedy looked at him and smiled. Greedy handed Vann the blunt and told him to have a seat. Greedy was still rapping, of course. After the song ended, he turned the radio off.

They all were finally together sitting at the table. Vann said wassup to Chase and Darren and then asked Greedy what was going on. Greedy was still smiling like nothing had ever happened.

"It's good to see you my nigga, fo' real. Real talk," Greedy told Vann. It was like he was trying to avoid everything that had just happened.

"It's good to see you too bro. What's up with you? You alright?" Vann asked while still looking for Greedy to give him some type of feedback.

"Man I hate to say it, but there's a lot going on with me right now that I just found out about," Greedy said. Darren then started thinking about Chenelle. He knew that there was something familiar about her. He thought about it again and again until it clicked.

"Oh shit Chenelle!" Darren was so fucked up from drinking beer that it actually didn't dawn on him, until now, that Chenelle was standing right in front of him earlier. And when she left, Greedy disappeared for a while too. Darren then put his head down and then he shook his head like how could he have been so stupid.

Chase was still hitting the blunt as Greedy was just about to explain to them why he was so upset. Then his cell phone rang. He looked down at his cell phone and saw that it was Gena calling him. When he saw that it was her, he turned his phone off. "Man I really don't want to talk to that hoe right

48

now, fo' real fool!" he told his friends.

"Who G?" Vann asked.

"Gena's bitch ass, that's who!" he said angrily. Vann was still so curious about why Greedy was so upset and had so much hostility built up inside. "Now, I have something important I need to tell y'all, and y'all might look at me different when I tell you this, but y'all my boys and this shit here is important," Greedy told them.

"Wassup man? Yeah we're your boys and shit. Anything you tell us, we are going to support you regardless of the situation. And that's real," Vann told him sounding agitated. Chase agreed and so did Darren.

"Aight...," Greedy then paused for a minute and then wiped his face. He was still a little nervous, but he proceeded on anyway. "You know o'girl who was just over here, right? Jewell's friend? Well we use to fuck around back in the H and she was saying that she might be pregnant and shit. But she wasn't. But, man she told me that she was tested for everything and then she told me that I was the one who gave her HIV." After telling his friends, Greedy stared straight at the wall.

"What tha fuck! Are you serious man?" Darren asked loudly while getting up from his chair. Vann looked at Greedy like how could this be happening. Chase was still hitting the blunt like he didn't even hear a word Greedy just said.

"Damn fool! How did you meet this girl? Did you already know her? What tha fuck is her name so I can stay tha fuck away from her?" Vann asked.

"Che' fool," Chase told him.

"Who in tha fuck is Che'?" Vann asked.

"Her name is Chenelle, and I...," Greedy didn't even get a chance to finish his sentence for getting cut off by Darren.

"Who? Chenelle! Damn!" Darren said. Vann looked up with the most disturbed look on his face. He just knew that Greedy wasn't talking about the Chenelle he was messing around with, and still was.

"Chenelle...light skinned, beautiful, luscious Chenelle...it couldn't be," Vann said.

"Yeah V, you know her?" Greedy asked.

"Yeah, I know her. She's an old friend of mine! DAMN! FUCK!" Vann said while holding his head. He couldn't believe what he was hearing; after he had just had sex with her the night before. Vann was really taking it hard. He didn't say much. He just told them that he would call them when he got to where he was going.

"What tha fuck is going on?" Greedy asked.

"Man, Chenelle is someone Vann use to talk to and they were suppose to have hooked up last night…Damn!" Darren said. Greedy was surprised, but he was determined to see who really gave him HIV.

"G, I'll be back fool. This nigga might be tripping too. Hey, and stay tha fuck away from Gena!
Go somewhere and chill for a min," Darren demanded as he walked out towards his car.

"Do you really think my sister gave you that shit fool?" Chase asked Greedy.

"Hell yeah I think she did. But all shit aside, I really don't know. I need to know who she's been fucking with tho," Greedy said.

"Damn this is some weird, fucked up shit!" Chase said while hitting the last of the blunt.

"Hey let's hit the strip. I need to see if Lace is up there. I have to give her these skittles," Greedy told Chase while popping a triple stack. Greedy didn't give a fuck before and he really didn't give a fuck now. He just had to tie up some loose ends with a few people that could have given him HIV. Normally, you would think that someone infected would hurry up and seek some medical attention; but not Greedy. He wanted some answers and he wanted revenge.

Heather Jornay Perkins

# Circles

## 5. I HAVE QUESTIONS AND I NEED ANSWERS

VANN DROVE HIS car as fast as he could, rushing towards Chenelle's hotel. While he was on his way there, he tried to call her but she never picked up. Vann was very disturbed and didn't care because Greedy couldn't have said it any better.

When he finally pulled up, he threw his car keys at the Valet Attendant and then found the quickest way to get to Chenelle's room; he hit the stairway. Reaching her floor and out of breath, Vann was still determined to get at Chenelle. He banged on the door like he was the police or the fire marshal. "Chenelle open tha fucking door!" Vann yelled.

The people in the hallway were looking at him like he was crazy. He was beating on Chenelle's door like he had no care in the world; and at this point, he didn't. After banging and banging on the door, Chenelle finally got up to see who was making all of that commotion. She was in a deep sleep and didn't hear him initially beating on the door.

As she got up, she slowly walked towards the door, "Who is it?" she asked.

"Chenelle open the door." Vann tried to keep it calm. Chenelle looked out of the peephole. Her eyes were still low from all of the crying she did earlier; on top of the fact that she had just woken up. But when she saw that it was Vann, her eyes widened. She could tell that Vann was upset and it threw her off because she had no idea why.

After she opened the door for Vann, he rushed in and slammed the door. Chenelle started stepping back as he grabbed her arms and started shaking her with a force that was to intentionally hurt her. Vann was questioning her, wanting to know why did she have sex with his homeboy Greedy. Chenelle looked so surprised. It shocked her when he mentioned Greedy's name. She had never seen Vann this upset and she had no idea that Greedy was his homeboy.

52

Vann pushed her on the bed. She fell knocking over the bottle of Blackberry Wine. "Bitch you heard what tha fuck I said!" Vann yelled.

Chenelle could barely speak after being shaken up by him. After she removed her hands from her face, she wiped her tears away. Chenelle screamed at Vann. She told him that she had no idea that Greedy was his homeboy and she had no good excuse as to why she had sex with him without telling him the truth. She couldn't explain herself at all. Vann was so hurt and angry that he could no longer look at Chenelle. Without another word, or any fight left in him, he just turned around and left her as she was.

When Vann finally made it back to his apartment, he checked his messages from earlier. One of them was from Trese letting him know to call her when he made it home. When he called her, she was chilling at her place, watching a movie and eating popcorn. Vann didn't know how to tell Trese what was going on, so he just kept quiet until he could figure something out.

Trese invited her man over and he politely accepted. Vann drove over to Trese's apartment not wanting to be alone at that moment. On his way there, he tried to call Greedy but he never reached him. Greedy's voicemail picked up so Vann left a short brief message.

It was around 11:00 p.m. and Greedy was up at Hard Body's Strip Club. He was looking for Lace, but he didn't see her. His whole purpose for coming out there was to get his money and Lace was the person to give it to him. Greedy sat down at the bar with Chase sipping on Hennessey and Coke. He couldn't help but to start thinking about the mess he was in with his girl Gena.

Gena went back to their house and packed up some things. She wasn't about to risk her life playing around with Greedy and his little games. She was scared of Greedy and what he could do to her. Gena was also confused because she knew that she would never jeopardize their relationship for anything. She was in love with him. She was so hurt because she could not believe that Greedy put his hands on her. That was enough to make her leave and stay with her mother for a while; at least until things got better between them. She still didn't know what was going on with Greedy but she was intending on finding out.

While leaving out the door, Gena called her brother Chase. Chase saw that Gena was calling him so he got up from the bar, leaving Greedy to tip the stripper who was giving him a lap dance. "What's up sis?" he asked her.

"What tha fuck is wrong with Greedy bro? Why was he tripping earlier?" Gena asked sounding hysterical.

"Sis, I can't talk about that shit right now. I'm with that nigga. Where you at?" Chase asked her.

"Tracie and Jewell taking me over to mama's," she answered.

"Oh…well…I'm ah get at you tomorrow, aight.," Chase told her.

"Um. Okay and make sure you do that," Gena said with an attitude.

Chase went back over to the bar where Greedy was still posted. Greedy asked him who he was talking to, but Chase didn't mention that it was Gena. He just told him that it was no one important.

Lace entered the strip club and Greedy noticed her as soon as she stepped foot in. He got up from the bar and started walking towards her. Chase was glad that he did because he knew that Greedy was about to drill him about who was calling. Greedy usually got like that whenever he was high. Greedy was rolling and when he approached Lace, he grabbed her with an aggressive kiss. "Damn boy! What you do that for?" Lace asked while trying to go around him.

Greedy wouldn't let her get by. He pulled her to the side by the restroom hallway and hemmed her up against the wall. "Wassup? You knew ah nigga was coming through; don't act like you didn't ask me to be here," he told her tight jawed.

"I know what I said nigga. Ain't nothing changed, but you high and you tripping kissing me like that and shit!" Lace told him.

"What? You have somebody up in here or something?" Greedy asked her.

"I might!" she said while trying to move away from him.

"Oh yeah that's what's up baby?" Greedy reached back

and pimped slap her without any hesitation. "Now! You have what up in here?" Greedy asked her again. Chase was watching Greedy the whole time. After seeing him slap Lace, he hurried and rushed over pulling Greedy away.

"Fuck you Greedy, o' hoe cake ass nigga!" Lace yelled, while holding her face in tears. Lace ran into the dressing room. Greedy was tripping with her fo' real. He didn't even care; he just laughed about the whole thing, although there was nothing funny at all.

Tremaine and his boys entered the strip club. They sat at a table near the bar where Greedy and Chase were sitting. Tremaine was very high and he was ready to start anything with anyone. Tremaine was the type of guy who always loved attention even though the ways in which he would get it wasn't always the way he intended.

He noticed Greedy leaving from Lace and kind of figured that something had went down between them because Lace was looking awkward and all. Lace feared that Tremaine was going to say something to Greedy, if he knew what really happened, and then have them all in a scuffle. She also knew that both of them were silly and ignorant, on the highest level, and they would not handle the matter in a mature manner at all.

Lace shook off what happened between her and Greedy and finished getting herself ready in the dressing room. Lace was not only messing around with Greedy, but she was also messing around with Tremaine. She liked that Tremaine was something like Greedy; he didn't give a fuck about anything and he didn't bow down to nobody, big or small. Lace wasn't really about Greedy though. She knew he was on that X and he would never be her man; just somebody she would get high with and occasionally mess around with. But on the other hand, Tremaine was different. She always kept in touch with him and she had been messing around with him for the past few months.


TREMAINE GOT UP from the table and asked one of the girls to go and get Lace for him. Lace quickly came out and hugged him tightly and then kissed him on the cheek. Lace was a real yellow bone and Tremaine could see that her face was plush red.

"What happened to your face baby?" he asked her. Lace didn't want to cause any trouble by telling him that Greedy was the one who made her face red. So she played it off and told him that she had been rubbing her face from it being irritated. Tremaine then looked at Lace straight in her eyes because he knew she was lying. He didn't ask her anything else about it and just rolled with it. He kissed her on the lips and then grabbed her butt and told her that she was leaving with him after the strip club.

While Tremaine was still with Lace, Greedy handed Chase the skittles to give to Lace. Chase walked to the back and saw Tremaine all up on Lace. When he approached them, he rudely interrupted them by handing Lace the skittles. Tremaine then looked at Chase like he had something on him. Lace smiled at Chase and then she took the pills to the dressing room to give to the other girls. Chase looked back at Tremaine and mugged him a little, showing Tremaine that he was no punk. As soon as Lace came back out Tremaine reminded her not to forget about what he said, and she nodded. She gave the money to Chase and before he left her sight, he told her to be careful because he knew how Greedy could get while he was rolling.

After Chase left, Tremaine gave Lace another kiss on the cheek. "I hope that hoe ass nigga didn't make yo face red Lace!" he told her. Tremaine knew that Chase wasn't the one who made Lace's face red, but that was just his way of trying to get something started on the cool. Chase didn't even bother to make eye contact with Tremaine; he was more concerned about Lace than trying to get into it with some niggas that he didn't even know. After Chase passed by Tremaine on his way back to the table with Greedy, Tremaine then walked back over to his table and left it at that. All the while, he really wanted Chase or Greedy to say something because he was ready for some drama.

Later on, things started to cool down, but Greedy was still rolling off the naked blue lady X he had popped earlier before hitting the strip club. While the strippers came out doing what they do, dancing for their money, Greedy and Chase made it rain with one hundred dollar bills, giving the strippers money for what they worked for. Besides all of the drama, Greedy had forgotten about everything else that was going on for that split moment.

It was finally time for the strip club to close up. Everyone went out to the parking lot to continue their mingling and some just left right after. Lace was standing out with her girls when Cool C pulled up in his 2008 Land Rover. He let his tinted window down and got Lace's attention. When she saw who it was, she went over to see him. She and Cool C had been friends for a long time. He really didn't want anything as he was just checking on her. They use to kick it before she started working at the strip club and before she started talking to Greedy and Tremaine. He handed her a roll of money because he always told her that he would look out for her no matter what the situation was. Lace started smiling real hard, as if she was blushing, after receiving the money. She thanked him and leaned over to give Cool C a peck on the cheek.

Cool C pulled off and then Tremaine came up to her and asked if she was ready to leave. Lace was more than ready, but before she left with Tremaine, she approached Greedy. "And what the hell was that all about in there, huh, Greedy?!" Lace asked him with anger in her voice. Lace was still upset with Greedy for slapping and embarrassing her.

"Man...," Greedy didn't have much to say to her. He was still high and loving the attention from all the strippers and especially Lace. Greedy knew he was wrong, but he took everything out on Lace that was bothering him.

"You know what Greedy! You're full of shit! Fuck you!" Lace told him. She really wanted to know why he was tripping with her earlier because it didn't make since to her at all. Greedy really didn't want to get into it so he brushed her off and then he and Chase burnt off.

Lace and Tremaine left and went back to her place in the Oakcliff. She had a three bedroom brick house that was fully furnished. She had everything that she needed and she worked for hers. Tremaine kicked his shoes off and then stretched out on the bed. "Boy your feet stank!" she told him while turning her nose up.

"Girl, my feet don't stank!" he said. They were laughing and tripping out, scoring on each other like little kids.

# Circles

Afterwards, Lace took a bath and then slipped into her T-shirt and panties. She laid beside Tremaine and started to rub on his chest.

"Baby, did you miss me?" she asked him.

Tremaine replied, "Yeah. I always do."

Lace started giggling, "Oh, you do, umm I like the sound of that."

"What are you laughing for? I'm serious girl. I mean, we've been good friends for such a long time and it's nice to know that we can still communicate like this with no problems, ya feel me?" Tremaine told her.

Lace then got on top of him, "Oh yeah, that's what I like to hear." Then she started kissing him slowly and softly on the lips and behind his ear because she knew that was his spot and that would get him aroused. He knew his girl Lace wanted to have sex with him. As soon as she hit the spot, it was like half time. The excitement just exploded and they had sex like they had never done before.

Meanwhile, Greedy and Chase crashed, back at his place, as soon as they made it through the door. Greedy's X pill binge had worn off and his body was feeling drained. Chase didn't have any problems getting comfortable and stretching out across the couch, calling it quits. While Chase was getting comfortable, Greedy couldn't wait to lay down himself. He went to the bathroom and washed his face with some warm water to relax some of the tension that he had.

After he washed his face, he took a couple of Advils and then went to his room and closed the door. He laid down on his bed and, as soon as his head touched his pillow, he fell asleep.

Heather Jornay Perkins

Circles

## 6. NEGATIVE OR POSITIVE

BY THE TIME morning came it was 7:31 a.m. and Vann was still over at Trese's place. He turned over and noticed that it was 29 minutes before 8:00 a.m., the time he scheduled his clinic appointment for. He was so relaxed with Trese that he forgot about the clinic appointment; it had totally slipped his mind. Vann ended up falling out of the bed which is what finally woke him up. He was trying to rush to put his clothes on, wide awake, and even still he was slipping out of the bed. When he finished putting on his clothes Trese giggled, "Baby, are you alright?" she asked.

"Yeah, I'm straight. I forgot I had an appointment this morning at 8 o'clock," he mentioned.

"Oh…where?" she asked.

"I will tell you later. I will call you when I'm done alright," Vann told her while walking out the door.

Trese was still in the bed. She didn't get up to lock the door until she heard Vann close it. Trese's phone began to ring and so she looked at it. It was Vann calling after he had already pulled off. "Yes," Trese answered her phone.

"Baby, we gunna have to do something tonight. Whatever you want, alright," he told her with such tenderness in his voice.

"Okay, baby," she agreed softly. They hung up and Vann rushed back to his place, took a shower, and then he headed towards the clinic.

At the clinic, there weren't too many people there since it was the weekend. The clinic didn't use to take patients on the weekends, but then they changed their hours to only allow for no more than 40 patients. This Saturday, Chenelle and Vann were both included in that group of 40.

Chenelle had already checked in and she was feeling a little nervous. She had already been seen back in Houston and the doctor prescribed her for a drug called Lexiva. She held on

to the prescription because she knew she had to see another
doctor to see what else was out there for her regarding the
medication that would be best for her.

She sat in the chair biting her nails, as she looked up
and noticed it was 8:10 a.m. While waiting, the receptionist had
Chenelle complete some paper work and then verify whether
or not she had the insurance that the clinic accepted.

After she completed all of the paper work, they made a
copy of her driver's license and then submitted her file back so
that the nurse could put her in line to be seen by the physician.
Chenelle patiently sat and waited until her name was called
next.

Vann arrived at the clinic at around 8:15. He checked
in and then took the clipboard of paper work that the
receptionist had given him and took a seat, not even looking
around to see who was in the waiting room with him. He just
sat down and started on his paper work.

Chenelle noticed Vann as soon as he entered the clinic;
he never noticed her. She stood up and walked back and sat
beside him. He looked up to see who was sitting next to him.
He looked at her, dead in her face, but did not say one word to
her. He just looked off as if he didn't even know who she was.

Vann finished his paper work and handed it back to the
lady at the front desk. Chenelle did the same thing along with
everyone else.

Chenelle got tired of sitting next to Vann in silence.
She decided that someone needed to say something so she felt
like she would make the first move. Just as she was about
to say something to Vann, her name was called, "Chenelle
Jones, Chenelle Jones," the nurse said in a loud voice. Chenelle
stood up and began to feel a bit fatigued and nauseated. As she
walked to the door, she fainted instantly. Vann didn't hesitate
as he jumped up and quickly ran to her side like nothing ever
happened between them. The nurse immediately took action
while another nurse assisted her. They rushed Chenelle to the
back in one of their rooms and laid her down on a bed table.
Vann wasn't allowed to go to the back with her, so he was very
frustrated. The doctor then came into the room with another
nurse and checked Chenelle's chart and her vital signs. Her
readings indicated that her blood pressure was up. The doctor

# Circles

then conducted an evaluation and then discussed the causes and effects of the HIV virus. He went into thorough detail. Afterwards, she told him about the medication that the doctor in Houston had given her. He was glad that she provided the information before she was injected with a double dose of medicine that wasn't needed until a few months later. So he just prescribed her some Lexiva, the same medicine that the other doctor prescribed her back in Houston. She received pamphlets and condoms before she left. Chenelle was feeling weak. The doctor told her that she had to keep up a healthy diet and drink plenty of fluids.

When she came out she didn't even bother to say anything to Vann. She didn't even look his way. Vann stared at Chenelle as she walked out without even telling him goodbye. He was confused, so he ran behind her before she could even walk out the building. "Chenelle!" he shouted.

She turned slowly with a frown on her face, "What?" she asked.

"What happened?" he asked her. Chenelle wasn't even in the mood to explain, so she just brushed Vann off real politely by telling him that she just needed to rest. Vann understood that she was tired. Before he let her go, he gave her a big bear hug. A tear fell from her face because she felt helpless towards her situation and all the people she had hurt.

Vann finally saw the doctor and was tested for everything. He received his results back from the STD testing but; for the HIV, it took three days. He was relieved that he had taken the steps to take the test, but he knew that the waiting part was going to be the hardest part. It made him even more stressed than before.

Chase's phone rang off the hook, but he didn't answer because he was in a deep sleep. Gena kept calling and calling. She was trying to reach her brother because she wanted to talk to him about everything since they still hadn't talked like they needed to. She really missed the times she and Chase had as children. When there was something wrong with her, she could always depend on at least talking to her brother before things had gotten out of hand with her situations. Gena, just didn't feel right until she expressed herself to him.

Greedy heard the phone ring and got up. He grabbed

Chase's phone and answered it not even checking the caller id
to see who it was. "Yeah!" he answered loudly.

"Yeah... who is this?" Gena asked.

"This Greedy, now who tha fuck is this?" he asked.

"Um. That figures," she said with an attitude.

"Oh yeah, Gena, so it's like that! Bitch stay where you at
hoe!" Greedy said. He was getting angry again so he hung up
the phone and turned it off.

He went to his room and threw on his clothes he had
on the night before. Greedy knew exactly where Gena was, and
he left heading her way. He was so upset because he thought
Gena was his girl. His delusional mind could not understand
why she didn't come home last night. Still thinking about the
HIV thing he didn't know what to do about the situation. All
he really wanted to know was who he got it from; who actually
gave it to him. If his hole couldn't get any deeper, he really
wanted to know if Gena was the one who gave it to him.

Greedy pulled up in front of her mother's house in
Oakcliff off of Kellogg. He took a last puff of his blunt and then
put it out. Gena looked out of the window to see who it was
pulling up in her mother's yard. "Mama! Tell me why this nigga
done came all the way over here!" Gena told her mother.

Her mother was in the back washing in the laundry
room, yelling, "I told you he would come Gena!"

Greedy rang the doorbell and Gena opened the door
letting him in.

"Hey, miss lady," Greedy spoke to Gena's mother.

Gena's mother was coming from the back, "Hey, Greedy.
Do I need to babysit you two or can I finish up my washing?"
she asked the both of them.

"Mama, you don't have to babysit. Greedy ain't stupid
to try anything!" Gena told her mother.

"Okay." Gena's mother walked to the back to finish her
washing. Greedy looked at Gena with his sad face and then sat
down on her mother's couch.

"So, are you gunna tell me why you flipped out on me
yesterday?" Gena asked him.

"Man..." Greedy sat back and tilted his head back with
his hands over his face. He really didn't know how to come at
Gena but he had no other choice.

# Circles

"Baby, I know I was wrong for acting a fool yesterday, but you just don't know what I've been going through for these last hours. Damn! Gena have you been fucking off on me?" Greedy asked her while balling his fist up.

"What? No I haven't! Have you?" she turned the tables on him by asking him the same question. Greedy then hesitated to even speak.

"Yes, I have. But, damn Gena it's deeper than that baby," he told her. Greedy then got down on his knees and started crying; he was breaking down. He grabbed Gena's hands and held them tightly. Gena didn't understand why he was acting the way he was. So she asked him why he was crying and what was really bothering him. Greedy finally cleared his throat and stood up and folded his arms, "Well you know the girl who came over last night for Jewell?"

"Yeah," Gena said.

"Well I met her when we all went out of town to Houston, a few months ago, and we messed around," he told her.

"Damn it Greedy! What tha fuck! Is she pregnant?" Gena shouted when asking him. Gena was so upset she couldn't even look at Greedy without wanting to slap the taste out of his mouth.

"No, baby, no. Listen she is not pregnant...," he assured her.

"Then what Greedy? What is so fucking important?" Gena asked.

Greedy just went ahead and let it all out. "Damn... she told me that she was infected with HIV." Gena slapped the taste out of his mouth. "Yeah, I deserve that!" he told her while rubbing the left side of his face trying to hold his composure.

"You bitch! I can't stand you Greedy!" Gena shouted. She was so upset and hurt that she went straight to her mother's room and grabbed the 38. She walked back to the living room and then pointed the gun straight at Greedy's head.

"You dirty ass muthafucka! How could you do this to me? How could you do this to us?" Gena was devastated. The gun clicked off of safety and Gena was still standing with the gun held towards Greedy head. She was ready to pull the trigger.

Gena's mother ran to the front when she heard all of the commotion, "Gena baby. Give mama the gun. Honey, give mama the gun." Her mother reached for the gun. Her mother was afraid of what Gena could have possibly done in just that instant. But Greedy didn't move. He just stood there still, wondering if Gena had the nerve to really pull the trigger. Her mother was actually afraid for Greedy because she knew that if he made one wrong move, in the state of mind Gena was in, he would've gotten shot.

"Gena I'm sorry, please forgive me. Please forgive me baby, please." Greedy was begging Gena to forgive him. Gena wasn't even trying to hear what Greedy was trying to say, but she did hear her mother asking for the gun. She then broke down and turned from Greedy and hugged her mother tightly, while sobbing in tears. Gena cried so hard that her mother couldn't do anything but hold her daughter and tell her that it was going to be okay and to trust in the Lord. Greedy knew it was the right time for him to leave so he slipped out without saying a word.

Making it back to his place, Chase was up playing the XBOX 360. He was really posted up too; serving all of his clients that cush. Greedy didn't say anything to Chase. He just walked right on by. He really wasn't feeling it at all. He turned his phone off and then laid back down on his bed.

After Chase finished the game he was playing, he took a shower, cleaned up a bit, and then left. He knew that Greedy had a lot on his plate, so he just left him to be by himself for a while. Chase went straight over to his mother's place to see how his sister was doing.

When Chase arrived, Gena told her brother everything that Greedy told her. Chase knew his sister wasn't doing his boy like that. He knew his sister was a better woman than that. Chase felt sorry for Gena. He knew that his sister didn't deserve what was happening to her. He stayed over to his mother's and chilled for a while and they all did a family prayer while he was there.

As soon as the shock and horror calmed down, Gena pulled herself together and scheduled an appointment through the automated system to be seen at the clinic. Her health was always top priority on her list. Thinking about everything that

was going on still sent chills and shockwaves through her
spine as she could not believe that she was exposed to HIV; and
exposed by her one and only true love. All she could do, at this
point, was wait and see if she was in waist deep. Having
this feeling made her look at everything differently and more
cautiously now. However, she found comfort in knowing that
she took a huge step with being proactive and making the
appointment to check her status.

Gena wasn't the only one feeling that pains of
nervousness and fear. Chenelle knew all too well what Gena
was feeling but was now going through a total new set of
anxiety because she now had to share the inevitable with her
family. She was typically confident in knowing the reactions she
would get from her family members; but this was a different
story. She was oblivious as to how they would feel or react to
her tragic news.

After leaving the clinic, Chenelle went over to her
parent's like she planned. Her mother was so happy to see her.
After Chenelle dropped the bomb on her mother, they hugged
and chatted as if Chenelle had never told her mother anything
was wrong. So, Chenelle just played along and that gave her a
little relief knowing that her mother wasn't looking at her in a
different way. Even though the news about the HIV was eating
her up inside, her mother had to put up a strong firm wall in
order to ignore the fact that her baby girl would actually die of
this disease one day. But, it was either dwell on the reality and
stay depressed or live for the day, and the moment, like it was
their last together.

It was Sunday, early in the afternoon, and her little
sister Chelsie was just getting out of dance practice. Her father
had just come back from his office at the church. Long before
they came, Chenelle had fallen asleep on the couch after she
and her mother talked about her childhood memories. She was
drained from the exhaustion of depression and the medication
her doctor had given her. Chenelle's mother didn't even
mention what was going on with Chenelle to her father. She
didn't know how, so she just waited for Chenelle to wake up so
they could talk about it then.

While Chenelle was stretched out on the couch, her
father kneeled over and kissed her on her forehead as he

Heather Jornay Perkins

headed towards the kitchen. Chenelle raised her head up and
smiled, "Thanks daddy."

Chenelle's mother was cooking up a good Sunday meal;
smothered pork chops, Mac & Cheese, greens, yams,
and cornbread. Her mother always threw down in the kitchen.
Chenelle figured that that was one of the main reasons why her
father married her; outside of the fact that they shared love at
first sight since high school. They were high school sweethearts
and, through their ups and downs, they still managed to keep it
together.

Chenelle was still resting comfortably on the sofa. She
really needed the rest to help relax her mind because she had so
much on it. She still needed to find a way to tell her father and
sister what was going on with her. However, resting was the last
thing on some other's minds.

Vann was drinking his worries away. "Baby is that
another Swamp Thing?" Trese asked Vann as she walked back
to the table coming from the restroom.

"Yeah it makes me feel a whole lot better baby, but you
know it's all good," he told her. Vann pulled Trese closer to him,
kissed her on the cheek, then on her neck, and, the next thing
you knew, they started making out inside the restaurant. Vann
couldn't help himself. He was a little tipsy and all he wanted
was Trese's body.

Trese knew her man was getting a little too excited after
his third drink. After he finished his third drink, Trese did not
let him order another drink. After he took his last sip, Trese
grabbed his arm and pulled him out the restaurant towards the
exit. "Baby, I wanted another drink! You act like I can't hold
my liquor! Trese, girrrl!" Vann said while tripping over his feet.
Trese started laughing. "Aww Trese. You laughing at ya boy
now! That's messed up and I thought we were better than that!"
Vann said while laughing too. After getting into the car they
headed back to her place. As soon as they walked through the
door, Vann didn't waste any time with her.

Vann had his way with her. He pushed her against the
wall by the door while grabbing her leg and lifting it. He
rubbed her thighs and kissed her lips aggressively. Trese liked
the aggression, but she had to slow Vann down a bit because he
was acting like something was bothering him. He was wasting

67

# Circles

no time getting down to business. When she tried to slow him down, it only made him want her even more. That was a turn on for her to say no or act like she didn't want it. He tore her blouse open and started to suck on her nipples, causing her to forget about the slowing down part. Trese was making slight moans, craving for more and more. Vann then laid her down on the living room floor and then spread her legs apart giving her what she wanted and what she needed.

He caressed her inner thighs working his way towards her vagina. Vann sucked and licked her clit making her body squirm and beg for more of the satisfaction. He licked from front to back, "Wow, baby you have never done this before," Trese told Vann while she was holding his head down with pressure and grinding on his face like she was riding his dick. She was trying to get the orgasm she wanted.

"Um, you like that baby?" Vann asked her while he was deeply into working his magic. Trese moaned and moaned; and she had got louder and louder as she began to climax all the while telling Vann to stop when she really meant for him to keep going. When Vann made her reach her orgasm, he slid his dick inside her and worked his way in making Trese say his name and whatever else was at the tip of her tongue.

After the rush of excitement, Vann pecked Trese on the lips, "Baby…," Vann hesitated while trying to catch his breath.

"What baby?" she asked him.

"Man you have me feeling things that I really couldn't even see in the beginning. You are my girl and I love being with you," Vann told her.

"Feeling what baby?" Trese asked playing like she didn't know. She knew Vann was feeling her a lot more than he did before. Vann looked into her eyes and said, "I love you Trese. I really do.

"Wow…you do baby?" Trese asked.

"Yes, I do. Trese baby, I've been feeling this way for a minute now, so how do you feel about that?" he asked her.

"Well, I feel the same way and you should already know that. I love you too, but I want more than just saying it. I want me and you to be together. Let's move in together!" Trese suggested to him. She thought her idea was a good one to suggest to Vann, but it was an ice breaker for him.

Vann's eyes got wide and he jumped up. He didn't say a word. He just looked surprised that Trese wanted to take it to the next level; and she wanted to do it so fast. It was like his life had flashed before his eyes; moving in together, getting married, and then having kids. That was a little bit too much for him to take in at one time and he didn't think about it before he opened up his big mouth.

He jumped up, looked at Trese all crazy, and then hurried and went to the bathroom. Trese was still lying down with a confused look on her face. She wasn't sure if Vann agreed to the suggestion or not. She thought, since Vann was opening up to her, that she could be more open with him too; but she now saw that it was the wrong thing to do. Even though they were feeling the same way, they were not ready to move in together, at least that's what Vann thought. He wasn't expecting her to say move in together. That was the last thing on his mind.

While Vann was still in the bathroom, he looked at himself in the mirror and stared at himself for a long time. He was in a daze thinking about why he had to sleep with Chenelle, when he knew he had a beautiful woman like Trese on his team. He knew he had messed up, but he was still hoping that things will be right.

Vann finally came out of the bathroom and picked his boxers up off the floor and slipped them on. Trese pulled the sheets off her bed and then wrapped herself up in them. She looked at Vann with the same confused look on her face after he had jumped up and ran out like something was wrong. They both sat down on the bed. Trese leaned over on Vann's shoulder, "Vann do you truly love me?"

"Yes, I do baby. Very much," Vann told her.

"Well, what's wrong? Why did you run out like that when I was only trying to open up to you?" she asked him.

"I don't know, I just…well you caught me by surprise when you said those things," he told her.

"Oh, I did?" she asked while sitting up.

"Baby I meant every word and I wouldn't say anything that I don't mean. But, moving in together is a bit too much, don't you think?" Vann asked.

"Well, I thought it was a great idea. I just missed you so

69

# Circles

much when we were apart; but, if that is how you feel then okay. I'm okay with that. Just remember that one day that time will come and you will still have to decide," Trese told Vann while smiling. Trese then stood up, bent down, and kissed Vann on his cheek. She went to the bathroom to take a shower.

After she walked out Vann looked in his pants pocket for his phone. He turned his phone on to check and see if he had any messages. He had four messages: one from Darren, one from Greedy, his mother, and his boss. Vann was really trying to see if Chenelle had called him, but she didn't. After checking his messages he went in the bathroom with Trese. It was extremely steamy. Trese liked her water very hot. Vann decided to join her in the shower, so he jumped in and, with the two of them in the shower together, well we all know what happened next.

Heather Jornay Perkins

Circles

## 7. THE DOWN FALL

BY THE SMELL of her mother's home cooking, Chenelle
finally got up and washed up for dinner. Her mother and father
were sitting at the table when Chenelle walked into the kitchen.
Her father gladly got up and gave his baby girl a nice warm
hug. Chenelle hugged him back and then asked where her
little sister was. Her sister was in her room on her cell phone,
Koolaiding as usual. Her mother sent Chenelle upstairs to get
her sister so they could enjoy dinner together as a family.

After enjoying dinner with her family, Chenelle told her
father and sister about her situation. When she explained
everything to them, she wasn't shocked by the way they reacted.
Her father was so emotionally distraught that Chenelle couldn't
take it so she excused herself from the table. It was so difficult
for Chenelle to accept their reactions that she had to leave the
house. She told her mother that she would stay in touch and
then kissed her father on his forehead and told them goodbye.
Chenelle went back to her hotel room. Although she was upset
to see how hurt her family was, she was also relieved that that
conversation was over. Outside of taking care of her own
health, telling her family was most important and she was glad
that she had gotten it out of the way.

Vann and Trese finished their shower and then Vann
left and went back to his place to finish up some paperwork
his boss had requested from him. Trese went over to Peaches'
and chilled. They played catch up for a couple of hours and
sipped on some of Peaches' famous pink panties. While Trese
was hanging, she received a call from Tremaine who she really
didn't want to talk to at the time. She declined his call and sent
him straight to her voicemail. She really wasn't feeling
Tremaine as her mind was more focused on Vann.

Tremaine was still at Lace's house just chilling and
letting time pass by. He was trying to see what Trese was up

72

to. By the way the ringtone changed, he could tell that she sent him straight to her voicemail. In retaliation, he sent her a fly text message, *How you gunna decline my call like that huh? That's wassup? You acting shady ma.*

Tremaine got up and got himself together so he could leave Lace's crib. He kissed her on the cheek and then burnt off in his 2007 Black Tahoe. He knew Trese was up to playing games, but he didn't sweat it because he knew that she would still need him for something.

Meanwhile, at 7:07 a.m., Monday morning, the police were surrounding Tracie's house. Quietly they approached the front porch and then pulled a kick door. They knocked down the door and immediately saw that it was a house full. The police had an outstanding warrant for Jewell. She was wanted for hot checks. Tracie and Keeno were in their room sleep and Jewell and her baby's daddy, Tank, were in their room. The living room was filled with teenagers and Tracie's and Jewell's kids. It appeared as though the kids had a sleep over.

Everyone woke up by the loud BOOM. The police were shouting, "Get up! Get up! Everyone up and against the wall! And don't move!" Keeno and Tracie both heard the laws and sprang up to attempt to get out of the bed. Just as they began to move, the police rushed in searching for their prime suspect, Jewell.

After they cleared the bedrooms, they had everyone on the wall with their legs spread apart, even the teenagers. The police had a search warrant so they searched the house looking for any type of evidence to throw on Jewell and whoever else was involved. "Look! Found something," one of the officers shouted from the back. They found printed checks and fake ID cards neatly laid out.

"Which one of you is Jewell Stephens?" one of the officers asked. It was silent and no one said a word. So the officer threatened to take everyone in and the kids to CPS if she didn't come forward. Tracie turned and looked at Jewell, but Jewell didn't budge. She didn't want to go to jail; she wasn't ready for all that.

"Bitch you better speak up. They know it's you," Tracie said in a low tone. The police officer smiled and then asked Tracie who she was talking to. Tracie didn't say anything; she

73

Circles

just glanced at Jewell. Then the police officer walked directly over to Jewell and asked her, "Are you Jewell Stephens?"

Jewell turned her head and looked at the officer and responded, "Yes, yes I am." Jewell said it with an attitude and the officer smiled and handcuffed Jewell and read her rights. The officer then frisked her and walked Jewell out of the house and put her in the police car.

After the other officers searched everyone and everything else, they found a lot of things that belonged to Tracie. They ran her name and found out that she had been wanted for a long time, but they just couldn't find her. Now Tracie's luck had finally run out, so they frisked and handcuffed her too. They were both taken to Lewsterret. The officers didn't harass anyone else. They had the one they were looking for. Coming across Tracie was a bonus.

Keeno and Tank were relieved. They both just knew that they were going down too, but the laws came and got who they wanted. Keeno wasn't tripping; he wasn't tripping at all. He knew what he had to do for his girl. He had to repay the same courtesy she did for him when he was locked up. However, until then, Keeno had to hold it down and come up with the money. He didn't hit the streets immediately though. He chilled and waited for a while to think of a game plan. While he was waiting, he spent sometime with his little girls and let them know that everything was going to be alright and that their mother would be home soon.

Around 11:45 a.m., Keeno made a few stops, and one of them just happened to be Tracie's brother, Greedy's, house. He thought Greedy should at least know about his sister being taken to jail.

Greedy was in the house knocked out, so Keeno didn't get an answer from him. He even tried to call him, but still there was no answer. The phone kept going straight to voicemail. He left a message telling Greedy to call him back ASAP. While sitting in his 2005 Lexus Coupe, Keeno rolled a blunt up and then started contemplating on how he was going to make some quick money to get Tracie out. Keeno also called Tracie's mother and told her about Tracie going to jail. He asked if she would come and get the girls because he needed to work on coming up with some money fast. Tracie's mother was already aware of the situation though. She had called her mother as soon as she made it in the holding tank. The situation her daughter was in wasn't new to her because she knew what kind of business Tracie and her friends were involved in. Her mother picked the girls up and decided that she was going to keep them until things got better with her daughter. Keeno gave her some money for the girls for the time being.

Once Keeno was relieved of the kids, it was time for him to move around and start making some things happen. He drove to Dixon Circle and went to his cousin Dre's crib. "Wassup nigga!" Dre said to Keeno while slapping hands with him. Dre was Keeno's little cousin. They grew up together off of Lagow in East Dallas.

"Shit, baby mama just got locked up," Keeno told him. Dre looked surprised because he had just seen Tracie and Jewell at Club Cirque just last night.

"Damn, fool fo' real!" he said while frowning.

"Yeah nigga. Them hoes came early this morning and bust the door down. Man that shit was crazy and too damn early in the fucking morning for that shit. Man everybody was there too. Now I got to hustle even harder. You know what I mean?" Keeno told him.

"Man, yeah I hear ya. Say if you need anything or any help, I got you my nigga," Dre said.

"Yeah, that's wassup young cuz. You good though," Keeno said.

Danny Boy bust through the door, "Dixon up in this bitch!"

"Ahhh! Wassup with ya boy?" Keeno asked him. Keeno was grinning from ear to ear; he hadn't seen Danny Boy in a minute.

Keeno, Dre, and Danny Boy had been around each other since elementary; it was like a reunion to have all of them together in the same room. They were just chilling and flipping money at the trap while letting time pass them by. Keeno was getting so high that he didn't slow down. All he wanted to do was forget about his worries with the mess that was going on at the time.

After kicking it in Dixon Circle at the trap, Keeno and

# Circles

Dre hit the streets to get rid of some more work they had. Keeno really wanted to be more on his grind than getting high, but that didn't play out like he wanted it to. Keeno was loaded, even though the plan was to grind for his baby girl. He had gotten so high that it was hard for him to stay focused on his priorities and Dre knew it. But, that was nothing new because Keeno got messed up all the time. He had a known drug problem and, by him selling, it wasn't helping the situation at all. However, Keeno was what one would consider to be a functional drug addict but Dre noticed that Keeno was acting a little different this time because his words started to slur and he was laughing at everything.

After Danny Boy left, Dre asked Keeno was he alright. "Man, nigga…am I aight. Shit, a real nigga can handle whatever the case maybe. Either you deal with the shit or you don't!" Keeno told Dre. It sounded like Keeno was more frustrated and angry than handling anything and being calm about it. Dre looked at Keeno with a look of concern, knowing that his big cousin was not being himself. Dre was even more so bothered when they headed outside to their cars.

Before getting into their cars, Dre was a little hesitant because he really didn't want Keeno to drive. But Keeno, being the hardhead he was, didn't want to listen so they both got into their cars and rolled out. It started to rain hard as soon as they pulled off. Keeno pulled up on the side of Dre and smiled. He was feeling so good that he didn't even realize that he hadn't put his seatbelt on as he sped to each stop. Dre tried to call him to tell him to slow down, but he couldn't hear his phone because the music was up so loud.

With each cross of a traffic light, Keeno accelerated even more. The roads were extremely slick from the rain. Right before he crossed the railroad tracks he hit a bump in the road that caused his car to skid and then flip over six times. Keeno was slung around and then thrown from his car and into the middle of the road. Cars stopped trying to avoid the accident. Keeno's body laid in the middle of the street, stretched out and lifeless. His car was on the other side of the street turned upside down.

Dre saw the whole thing and couldn't believe what was before his eyes. Dre hurried up and parked. He got out his car and immediately rushed over to Keeno and called 9-1-1. Cars stopped and people rushed over to see if everything was okay, but it didn't look as if it was. Dre checked for Keeno's pulse, but there was nothing. Dre just knew the unthinkable wasn't happening; but it was. He knew it was all over for his cousin and it happened so quickly; right before his eyes could blink. The pain hit him instantly and Dre started crying and screaming real hard.

As soon as the ambulance and police arrived, they rushed over quickly to Keeno's motionless body. Dre was still holding Keeno in his arms when the police walked up and asked Dre if he could come with them to discuss the incident. The paramedics put Keeno on a stretcher, rushed him into the ambulance, and placed an oxygen mask on him. There were no vital signs left in Keeno; he was gone.

The police questioned Dre wanting to know what caused the accident. He told them what he saw as well as some of the other witnesses. Just so happen, Gena and Chase were passing by while all of the commotion from the accident was going on. Gena's eyes got big when she saw Keeno's car. "Damn, Chase look!" she said.

"What?" he asked.

"Pull over! Pull over!" Gena shouted hysterically. She and Chase jumped out the car where they saw all the people standing around. But they still couldn't see exactly what was going on. When they got a little closer, they could see Keeno's body being placed inside the ambulance and that his car was totaled. Tears immediately started rolling down Gena's face. They saw Dre talking to the police, so they walked over to see how the accident happened. Gena didn't know what to think, so she asked Dre if Keeno was still alive. Dre responded with a whispering *no*.

After the police completed their conversation with Dre, he walked back to his car slowly with his head down. Chase and Gena walked with him and that's when Dre told them exactly what happened and how high Keeno was. "Man it was crazy. Keeno was driving faster than a bitch! He pulled up on the side of me and smiled and I was trying to tell him to slow his ass down, but he didn't. After he pulled off, man it was like I knew something was about to happen. As soon as he pulled off it was like a bright shining light was over him and, before I knew it, he flipped over and over and over."

Dre burst out in tears again. Gena held him, "Man, it's going to be okay Dre." Gena was hurt herself and Chase was more shocked than he was hurt. After Dre told them what happened, he walked away in silence. He knew that he needed to hit the block and tell the rest of the homies about what happened. Dre was feeling like it was his fault because he knew Keeno was messed up from the jump, but Keeno would have never listened to him because he was too bullheaded; especially when he was fucked up.

Before driving away, Dre sat back in his car and thought about how everything happened so quickly. He couldn't hold it in any longer. He began to scream and cry. He cried like he never had before. He had lost associates from the neighborhood but he had never lost anyone close to him like his big cousin, Keeno. This really messed his head up.

After Dre left, Chase and Gena pulled off right behind him and went over to Greedy's place to give him the bad news. Gena had felt like she needed to be the one to tell him since that was his sister's baby's daddy and all. She thought someone close to him should be the person to tell him and she knew that it was her place to do so.

WHEN THEY FINALLY made it to Greedy's place, they pulled into the driveway. When they walked in, they noticed how abnormally quiet it was. Greedy's cars were parked in the front so they knew he was there. Greedy was in the back room sleeping. Chase didn't even bother going back there. He went straight to the kitchen and fixed himself something to eat, while Gena went to the backroom where Greedy was.

When she walked through the bedroom door, she saw Greedy bundled up in his covers asleep. She tried to be as quiet as possible, not wanting to wake him just yet. She sat beside him and tapped him on his shoulder. Greedy must have been sleeping real good because he didn't respond. Gena wasn't in the mood to deal with his attitude so she gave up for a minute and laid beside him for a while.

After about an hour passed, Greedy rolled over and noticed that Gena was on the side of him. He smiled and then kissed her on the forehead. Before Greedy rose up to get out of bed, Gena opened her eyes and turned around to look at him. "Greedy!" Gena said. He looked at her and asked her what she was doing back at the house. She was very hesitant about how she was going to let him know about what just happened.

"Well…," she said while looking down and playing with the pillow that was in her lap.

"Well, what Gena? What's wrong?" Greedy asked her sounding very concerned. After all they had been through earlier, he didn't know how to act or what to expect. Gena just came out with it.

"Keeno died today," she told him. That was the only thing that could come out of her mouth.

"What!?" he replied.

"Keeno died today baby," she repeated.

"Are you fo' real Gena? Don't play with me," he demanded.

"I'm not playing Greedy, I'm serious," Gena expressed.

"Where your brother at?" he asked.

"He's in there," she said. Greedy couldn't believe that Keeno was gone.

Greedy got out of the bed and headed to the front to find Chase. When he made it to the living room, he saw a napkin with crumbs on it lying next to Chase. He had fallen asleep on the couch. Greedy shook him hard and woke him up.

"Say bro, Keeno gone my nigga?" Greedy asked Chase.

"Yeah," Chase said while rubbing his eyes. Chase was the type who really didn't like to talk about emotional shit. And lately, that's all the conversation he was having; emotional shit.

"Did anyone tell my sister or my mama?" he asked them.

"No…well we didn't. We thought we would tell you first so you could," Gena said. Greedy didn't waste any time. He slipped his shoes on and grabbed his keys. He left quickly and headed straight towards Tracie's crib.

When he arrived at his sister's place, he didn't get an answer so he figured they were all at the hospital. Greedy tried calling her, but her phone just kept going to voicemail. So he went over to his mother's house. He wasn't sure if she knew about what happened to Keeno.

# Circles

As soon as he made it into the parking lot, his every movement was timed very slowly. He didn't know how he was going to tell his mother or his nieces about what happened to their father. Opening the door with his key, that his mother had given to him a while back, he walked right on in. "Uncle, Uncle, Uncle!" his nieces shouted with excitement in their voices. They were very happy to see Greedy.

"Hey ya'll! What's good; tell your Unc something good?" Greedy asked them.

"Nothing," they both said while smiling. Greedy's mother then came out of the kitchen and gave her son a big hug.

"Mmmmm. Hey baby. How you been?" she asked him.

"I'm fine mama. Can I talk to you for a minute?" Greedy asked her.

"Sure. Let's go into the kitchen. I'm cooking," she told him as she led him into the kitchen. Greedy took a seat at the kitchen table and he watched his mother stir up her Hamburger Helper. He smiled and then placed his hand over his mouth and closed his eyes. When Greedy's mother turned around, Greedy's eyes were still closed tight. She sat down, "What's bothering you baby? Are you hungry because you know that you love my Hamburger Helper?"

Greedy smiled and then grabbed his mother's hands, "Nah, mama, I'm good."

"So what did you have to talk to me about? Is it about your sister going to jail because I already know about that," she told him. Greedy was shocked. He didn't even know that his sister had gone to jail. His mother told him what happened and that's why the girls were over. Now, it was even harder than he thought it would be to tell her what happened to Keeno; but he knew it had to be done.

"Mama, Keeno just died in a car accident," Greedy told her.

"Huh... What?" she asked.

"Yeah, ma... Keeno is gone," Greedy said again. She pulled away from him and then stood up and walked over to her pot of Hamburger Helper. As she stirred and stirred, tears started to quickly roll down her face. Greedy knew that his mom would be hurt after she heard that kind of news. So he got up and wrapped his arms around her tightly.

And that's when Greedy took everything in at once and then broke down. He was thinking about how all this time, while he was sleeping, a lot had happened. Greedy's heart was in pain and his mother couldn't believe how hard he was taking everything and that she had to be strong for him and her grandbabies. She turned to him, gave him a long hug, and talked to him. She told him that the Lord doesn't make mistakes and he has a pattern that is designed for everyone. Greedy knew that what she was telling him was true, but he just couldn't understand why now.

After talking to his mother he left and drove around for a bit. He left his mother's house feeling worse than he felt before. He felt as though he should have shared his own problems with his mother. Maybe that would have relieved him some and he could have received a word or two for his own life.

After driving and driving, Greedy found himself in front of Lace's house. After everything had sunk in, he thought it was time for someone else to suffer. The reality of his own problem set back in and he was overcome with the feeling of revenge and hate. He couldn't even look his mother in her face and tell her the truth and somebody needed to pay. In his mind, there was only one person that could have given it to him and all he could think about was Lace.

Circles

## 8. OUT OF CONTROL

GREEDY SAT IN his car for a while before getting out. He smoked a blunt and then called Darren up. "Wassup nigga!" Greedy said.

"Shit nothin' much, not much at all. Just about to leave the J-O-B," Darren told him.

Greedy took a last hit from his blunt and then started telling Darren what happened to his sister and Keeno. Darren couldn't believe what he was hearing and Greedy still couldn't believe it himself. Darren then asked Greedy if he was okay and where he was at. Greedy didn't respond, so Darren asked him again. Greedy was hesitant to even let Darren know where he was. When he told him he was in front of Lace's house, Darren asked him why he was over there. Greedy then quickly responded, "Man this is the bitch who gave me that shit!" Greedy was so angry and Darren knew Greedy wasn't in his right mind. He didn't want Greedy to do something that he knew he would regret for the rest of his life.

"Say calm down bro. I know you want to confront this bitch right now, but look, there is too much going on right now. Now is not the time G. I know you don't want to do her like that…you not right fool," Darren told him.

"My nigga, you don't know how I'm feeling! My mind is so fucked up right now. So much shit has been going on to me and my family. I have no reason to live fool!" Greedy said in the most disturbing tone. Greedy then put the phone down and reached for his gun which was in the glove compartment.

"Greedy…Greedy! Damn fool! Fool you tripping right now!" Darren was shouting over the phone trying to get Greedy's attention, but Greedy was already in action. When he realized that Greedy was no longer on the phone, he hung up and called Vann because he didn't have a clue where Lace lived; however, Vann did.

## Heather Jornay Perkins

Greedy grabbed his gun and stuffed it in the back of his pants. He got out of the car and walked towards Lace's front door. Lace was already looking out of the window at Greedy. Before he even had a chance to ring the doorbell, she opened the door already talking crazy and asking him what he was doing at her house. Greedy then put on the fakest smile and then forced his way in. "Greedy what are you doing here?" Lace asked him again. Lace had her nightgown still on because she hadn't planned on doing anything but lounging for the day.

"Girl stop tripping you know why I'm here," Greedy told her while yanking her hair and pulling her close to him.

"Greedy you're hurting me," Lace started to whine.

"Oh yeah? I'm hurting you? Well then bitch, I guess we're even because you have already hurt me. Now...it's my turn." Greedy threw Lace on the floor and opened her legs and forced himself inside her; jamming harder and harder until she cried for him to stop. After Greedy finished raping her, he then pulled the trigger leaving her in silence.

Darren and Vann finally pulled up, although a little too late. Greedy had already done his damage and it was a mess. Greedy sat on the floor against the wall with the gun still in his hand as Lace laid in a puddle of blood.

When Darren and Vann approached Lace's front door, they knocked and knocked with each knock getting harder and harder. But there was no answer. In a final attempt to gain entry into the home, Darren turned the door knob and surprisingly the door was unlocked; so they let themselves in.

"What tha fuck!" Vann said while closing the door in horror.

"Greedy give me the gun," Darren calmly told Greedy in an attempt to keep him from doing something else stupid.

Vann grabbed a towel out of the bathroom and rushed back to retrieve the gun from Greedy. Greedy slowly gave him the gun. Then Vann reluctantly called 911. He didn't want to have to do it but he had no other choice. If he didn't call the police then it would have looked as if they were trying to cover up for Greedy.

"Fuck, G! You've fucked up man!" Darren screamed.

"Why did you have to kill her? Why? This shit just doesn't make any since my nigga!" Vann told him.

# Circles

It was as though Greedy was in his own little world. He didn't move at all. Tears just began rolling down his face. His clothes were dirty from the blood stains and everything that Vann and Darren were saying to him was coming in a blur. He was so shaken up that he just looked up and asked Vann and Darren, "What happened and why is Lace laying on the floor?" Vann and Darren looked at Greedy with confusion. They couldn't understand why he was asking questions about a crime he had just committed.

Before they had a chance to even respond, the police busted in and immediately told all of them to get on the wall. Vann and Darren quickly did as they were told but Greedy was still out of it so he didn't move. The police instructed Greedy to get against the wall one more time. When he did not move, they pinned him to the floor and the other policemen took Vann and Darren out of the house. The paramedics rushed inside and to Lace's blood soaked body.

Once all of them were outside, detectives began to question Vann and Darren about the incident. "We just got here. Our homeboy was already here. When we went inside and saw that he had killed someone, we called the police," Vann said.

"How do you know that he killed this young lady?" the detective asked them.

"Because, when we got here she was laying in a puddle of blood and Greedy had the gun still in his hand," Darren told him while holding his head down in confusion.

"Okay. Where is the gun?" the detective asked.

"I took it; but I didn't touch it. It's wrapped in that yellow towel in the house." Darren was getting so upset that he to told the detective to ask Greedy because that's all that they knew.

The detective looked at Darren with a frown on his face because he knew Darren was trying to be smart. "Now look here son, what is your name?" the detective asked.

"Darren," he told him as he looked down at the ground.

"Okay, Darren this is standard procedure for me. I ask the questions and you give me the answers. You can either do that or I can make you cooperate downtown," the detective said.

84

"Yeah...," Darren mumbled in a low tone. This is a big thing, and the detective did not have time to play around because it was a serious matter. Darren understood and Vann did too. So any other questions the detective had, they answered and gave their personal information to them too because they were at the scene of the crime.

After the detective finished questioning them, Vann and Darren walked away before things became even more awkward for them; on top of the fact that they didn't have a lawyer to represent them at that time. So they moved quickly after they were done with the Q&A session.

When Vann finally made it back to his apartment parking lot, he sat in his car and thought about what just happened. He couldn't believe how things had gotten so far out of control. He couldn't wait to call Chenelle to tell her everything that had gone on.

When he spoke to her, she couldn't believe it. She was shocked that she was being blamed for the whole situation. "Damn this...man this is crazy Chenelle! You came back here and got all of this shit started up. Everything was cool before you came back. Damn!" Vann was getting even more upset just thinking about how the whole thing popped off.

"Hold up! Don't you point your finger at me like I'm the bad person! I'm the one who was surprised and hurt by what the nurse and doctors told me; that I'm infected with this disease! Now before anything else comes out of your mouth, you put yourself in my situation and then you let me know what was the best thing to do!" Chenelle snapped.

"Chenelle, the shit done already happened! Cuz yo mutha fucking ass did me that way, but it was worst because you weren't going to tell me and that's fucked up! Fuck, what you talking about?!" Vann said as he hung up in her face. Vann was highly pissed off at Chenelle because she was still the same person; selfish and thought about herself only.

When Vann finished jumping down Chenelle's throat, he tried to call Darren, but Darren was too busy to pick up the phone at the time because he was at Greedy's mother's house. She had been receiving bad news all day and now this. Darren had more bad news to give her as if she could take anymore.

As soon as Darren told her the news, she dropped to

her knees and broke down in tears. She cried so hard that Darren wrapped his arms around her and held her. "Don't worry Ms. G. The Lord will handle this," Darren told her.

"I know, I know. I want to believe that this storm will pass, but I'm too weak now to even believe anymore. Darren I've been trying to be the backbone and be strong for my family, but this...this is more than I can handle."

Darren continued to hold Ms. G. "I know. I know, Ms. G. I'm here." The bad news was just spreading so quickly about Greedy killing Lace. Now since the bad news had reached Greedy's mother, Gena and Chase were in for another shocking depression.

The next morning Vann received his results back from the clinic while Gena decided to finally go into a clinic to get tested. The news about his HIV was out and sent Vann into shock. He was in his living room sitting on the edge of his couch holding his cell phone to his ear listening to his results of his HIV testing. "Yes! Hell yes!" Vann shouted. The nurse told him that his test came back negative and he was more than relieved; he felt blessed.

He was supposed to be at work at 10:00 a.m., but he was so elated that he decided to go in at 9:00 a.m. On his way to the workplace he called Trese.

"Hey baby girl," Vann said. "Hey baby," Trese replied.

"Can we get some alone time tonight? I mean that's if you don't mind being with your man and all," Vann asked her. He was so happy that his results were negative that he figured there was no reason to tell Trese anything. He was just ready to move forward and avoid making the same mistake twice.

"Oh trust, I don't mind. And I'm glad you asked because I want to talk to you about something," Trese told him.

"About what baby?" Vann had a confused look on his face.

"I'm not gunna get into that right now, later ok," she said.

"Aight, I'm ah hit you up later," Vann said.

"Okay baby," Trese said while hanging up the line. Trese had a lot on her mind and she really needed to talk to Vann and get some things off of her chest. She wanted her relationship with Vann to work and last, but there were just some things that she wanted to clarify. She knew she had a good man, but she wanted him to be truthful and honest with her; to be real with her rather than being fake.

Vann finally made it to work and Darren was already there. He went into Darren's office and told him the good news and boy was Darren happy to hear that his boy was ok. "Any word on Greedy?" Vann asked Darren. Vann leaned against Darren's desk and folded his arms.

"Man, last I heard was that they had to put that nigga in a cell by himself; shit he was clowning down there," Darren told him.

"Damn fo' real! That nigga taking that shit hard. I mean he should; he did just kill an innocent person," Vann said.

"Well yeah, but what would you have expected from him when after finding out that he had HIV. Apparently he knew that Lace was the one who gave it to him. That's why he killed her. Then he turned around and gave it to Chenelle not knowing that he had the shit. And now Gena might have it too. Honestly, with that nigga, the shit can go on and on," Darren told Vann. Darren was in denial about the situation and taking up for Greedy; but Vann thought of it so differently.

"Yeah, that's a little too ill for me. I mean for that nigga to get caught up like that," Vann then stood up and started walking towards the door.

"Yeah, that's some ill shit," Darren agreed.

"Aight. Well I'ma hit you up for lunch," Vann said while making his way out of Darren's office.

"Aight," Darren said. Vann went on to his office. Once he made it to his office, he walked directly over to his desk and sat in his chair. He then glanced at his picture of Trese and smiled. Good things started flowing in his mind.

While Vann spent his time thinking of Trese, she on the other hand, was not spending her time thinking of Vann. Trese was at home on the phone with Tremaine. The conversation they were having gave Trese a lot of information which she was left out in the dark on. "Trese, this stripper I knew back in the day got killed the other day. Man, that shit fucked me up!" Tremaine told her.

"What happened to her? Who was she?" Trese started asking questions wanting to know more.

# Circles

"Her name was Lace, she was just a known stripper that everyone knew and this nigga named Greedy went to her house and killed the girl!" Tremaine said.

"Damn fo' real! Are you sure it was Greedy?" Trese asked him.

"Yeah, why you know this nigga?" he asked her.

"Hell yeah! That's my man's homeboy and he hasn't even mentioned it to me," Trese said.

"Damn!" Tremaine said.

"So, do you know why he killed her?" she asked.

"Shit something about she gave that nigga HIV and shit, but I heard that it was his old fling. Some chic name Chenelle," he told her.

"What!? Are you serious? That is some crazy shit fo' real Tremaine!" Trese exclaimed.

"Yeah it is, but ah…Trese I need to see you. So when you gunna let me see you?" Tremaine asked.

"Well, I don't know. It can't be today; my nigga wants to chill with me, but I will let you know," she told him.

"Aight, just don't make me wait too long," he said.

"Boy, I won't," she told him.

After Trese hung up, she laid back down and fell asleep. Before she fell asleep, she thought about Vann and what could have possibly been the reason why he failed to mention the murder and Greedy's involvement and Chenelle. Trese knew that was his ex girl back in the day, so she thought that Vann could have at least talked to her about something that's so serious.

After Trese fell into a deep sleep, she started to dream about Vann and this woman who she couldn't identify. They were having sex and then all of a sudden she was in the closet and some shoes fell. A letter fell out of one of the shoes and Trese couldn't really make out what the letter was saying. After the noise Trese made in the closet, Vann and the woman looked at the closet and that's when Trese woke up. She felt like the dream was real; too real. The dreamed disturbed her beyond belief.

She called up Peaches and told her about the dream she had had. "Girl that's a crazy dream. So you and Vann been okay? Has he told you anything for you to feel that way?"

Peaches asked Trese.

"Uh uh, but girl later on we are suppose to be spending some time together and that's when I will try to get something out of him," she told Peaches.

"Do you think your dream is trying to tell you something?" Peaches asked.

"Umm. I really can't say. But, I hope not and...," Trese's other line clicked. It was Vann.

"Peaches, let me call you right back, okay."

"Alright. And call me right back Trese," Peaches demanded. Trese hung Peaches up and clicked over to Vann.

While Trese was attempting to hang Peaches up, his other line rang and he saw that it was Chenelle. The second Trese clicked over to Vann, he clicked over his line over to Chenelle.

"Hey," she said softly.

"Oh, wassup girl. I got my results back," Vann told her.

"You did. From the way you sound I can tell it was some good news huh?" Chenelle asked.

"Ahhhh, yeah. But, I'ma hit you back aight," Vann told her.

"Okay that's cool," she said.

When Vann clicked back over, Trese had already hung up. So, Vann hurried and hit speed dial because he knew how Trese was. But little did Vann know, Trese was not trying to be on that level like he thought she would be. When Vann called her back, he got her voicemail. So he left a message explaining why he didn't click back over.


MEANWHILE ON THE other side of town, Gena went to her appointment to get a pregnancy test, STD's test, and an HIV. Gena still couldn't believe the things that were happening to her; especially having to deal with the possibility of having to live with this sickly virus. She felt as though she was at a standstill at this point in her life. The nurse told her that her results for the HIV test would be back within 3 business days. All of her other test were okay and she wasn't pregnant. *Thank God I'm not pregnant*, Gena said to herself.

# Circles

While Gena was at the clinic finishing up, Greedy was under investigation for the murder of Lace. The first time Greedy was interrogated, he was fully determined to tell the detectives all that he knew, which was the truth of why he did what he did. He was very calm and didn't waste any time telling them why he killed Lace.

The detective walked in with a folder in his right hand and a cup of coffee in his left. He laid the folder on the table, and then took a sip out of his cup. All of this time Greedy was watching the detective's every move. After the detective looked in the file, which was created for Greedy, he looked up and stared Greedy in the eyes. "Gerald...or do you prefer Greedy?

As soon as Greedy was about to answer, the detective interrupted him. "Don't answer that because I'm going to call you Gerald; only because that's what I want to call you. Now isn't that how you felt when you made it up in your mind to kill that poor girl?"

"Yeah...yeah I did and you're right. I did it because I wanted to," Greedy told him. The detective was shocked to see that Greedy was acting all nonchalant and showing no emotion what so ever. The only reason why Greedy didn't show any emotions was because he didn't want anyone to see him breakdown from the guilt that he was feeling. He wished that he could go back and change what he had done, but he couldn't.

Once the word got out, no one could believe that Greedy had killed Lace. When the autopsy report came back, a confirmation was provided to Lace's family, and Greedy, that she was infected with the HIV virus.

Greedy's mother really didn't know exactly what was going on; she was blindsided by everything and was too confused to piece things together. She decided to go and talk to someone who could possibly help her out. She contacted Gena's mother who filled her in on everything. Greedy's mother was flabbergasted yet still couldn't understand why her son did so much and never came to her with any of the things he was going through. She began to cry all over again. She knew her son was better than this. She would have never expected anything like this from her son.

As Greedy's mother continued to talk to Gena's mother,

Gena walked through the door. "Gena what happened? Did everything turn out okay?" her mother asked with concern. Gena flopped down on the recliner next to the window and gazed out of it like she had a lot on her mind.

"Mama if you're talking about the HIV test, then no. I didn't get the results back today and they won't be back for 3 business days," Gena told her. She noticed that Greedy's mother was there, so she spoke and gave her a hug.

"Oh, ok. I was just wondering. I was talking to Ms. G and filling her in with the news about everything," she replied back to Gena.

After Gena gave Ms. G a hug, Ms. G asked to speak to Gena alone. "Do you mind if I speak to Gena alone for a moment?" she asked Gena's mother just out of respect. Gena's mother nodded yes and then walked to the back leaving Ms. G and Gena alone to talk.

Greedy's mother really didn't go into detail with her about the whole situation because she knew Gena was hurting more than anyone. She just wanted Gena to know that she was there for her and that she could come to her for anything. She even apologized for Greedy's faults and what he put her through. But, that was the least of Gena's concern. She could have cared less whether or not Greedy's mom was there for her. All she wanted, or prayed, was for her test to come back negative and to know that she was going to be okay. The words that were coming from Greedy's mother's mouth actually went through one ear and out the other.

The phone started to ring in the back and Gena's mother picked up. It was Greedy. "Hey mama," Greedy said.

"Hey. Now, let me tell you something; I know people make mistakes. But Greedy, this is a mistake that you cannot fix. I love you still and I want you to know that whatever you're going through now, the ones who truly love you are hurting the most. The only thing that you can do now is ask God for forgiveness. Now, I'm going to get Gena for you okay," Gena's mother told him. Greedy took what she said to heart because he knew exactly what she meant and that she meant every word she said to him.

Gena got on the phone and the conversation got heated as soon as she started talking. "Why did you fuck up? Come on Greedy you're better than that; at least that what my brother and I thought. I don't know how we were the one's to get into this predicament. She started crying; it was killing her to even continue talking to Greedy. Her feelings were shattered into pieces.

"Baby, I know there is no excuse or explanation for what I did and what I'm putting you through, but...," Greedy couldn't even finish his sentence before Gena interrupted him.

"But, what? Huh Greedy?! Fucking up and then forgiving you and then you fuck up again. You did this! I can't even talk to you right now! I can't talk to you!" Gena said as she threw the phone down and started crying.

"Gena! Gena! Pick up the fucking phone! Damn! This is some bullshit!" Greedy was yelling and cursing. He didn't want to lose Gena at all. But little did he know, he had already lost her. Gena heard him screaming; however, instead of answering him, she left the phone on the floor and went to her room.

She laid down and her mother came into the room to see if Greedy was still on the line but he had already hung up. Greedy's mother wanted to talk to him too, but he hung up too soon to even know she was there.

Trese turned her phone back on after it had been fully charged. Even, though she didn't have to keep it off while it was charging, she did anyway so she could think. Trese had a lot on her mind. She couldn't wait for her evening with Vann because she had a lot on her mind and, thanks to Tremaine, she knew more than she was suppose to know. She went through her messages on her voicemail. "This fool has to be the best liar ever," she said out loud. She had a smile on her face because she knew Vann thought he had her where he wanted her. But leaving her those sweet messages didn't work because she couldn't trust him after thinking about what Tremaine told her earlier. It really bothered her that Vann never mentioned any of it to her. She wanted to spend quality time with Vann, but couldn't because it wouldn't feel right. Trese would still think about why Vann didn't mention anything to her. But that was the least of her worries because Tremaine wasn't being totally honest himself. He still hadn't told Trese that he too slept with Lace a few times and not too long before she was killed.

Heather Jornay Perkins

# Circles

## 9. TRYING TO GET THROUGH IT

IT WAS GETTING later in the evening and Trese was getting ready to meet up with Vann. She made herself look really nice and she put on some Escape because she knew that Vann couldn't resist that perfume on her.

While she was getting herself together, Vann was at his crib setting the mood just right for his baby; from making sure his apartment was nice and clean, to lighting candles, to laying out rose petals on the bed, to a hot bubble bath, to some Isley Brothers playing in the background, and to the chocolate sweets he had for Trese. He knew Trese loved Hershey Kisses so he had a bowl of them along with some strawberry syrup and whip cream right next to the bed. Vann had the whole night planned and wasn't expecting any interruptions.

He got himself ready and when he placed his last drop of cologne on his neck, there was a knock on the door. "Yeah be there in a sec!" he yelled. However, on the other side of the door was Chenelle waiting for Vann to answer. Vann just knew it was Trese getting there a little bit early. He opened the door, and when he saw who it was, he quickly slammed the door back. "Damn Chenelle! What are you doing here?" Vann asked her while the door was still closed.

"Vann I was just coming by to tell you that I was on my way back to Houston. I just wanted to see you before I left, that's all," Chenelle told him. Vann opened the door, but he didn't invite her in because he knew if he did things would have been a little different. Even though Chenelle was infected with the virus, Vann still cared for her and was still attracted to her.

"Oh ok I thought…," Vann started to say before he was interrupted.

Chenelle moved closer to him. "You thought what?" Chenelle asked him. As soon as she moved in closer to him, Vann couldn't resist her. She leaned in and gave him a kiss on the lips and, before you knew it, Vann kissed her back like he didn't even have plans with Trese. He stopped before things heated up too much and then kissed Chenelle on her forehead. "Well, that's all I wanted. And you look nice. Tell Trese to enjoy what she has because I know I did." Chenelle smiled as she walked away.

"Say how did you know my girl's name?" Vann asked her before she walked away.

"Oh. There are people and ways. Information does travel boo boo," she told him. Chenelle and Vann closed their conversation and then Chenelle finally left.

When Trese was turning into the parking lot, Chenelle was walking down the sidewalk and Vann had already closed the door. Trese really didn't suspect anything when she saw Chenelle. They both made eye contact and didn't think anything of it. Chenelle got into her car and drove off and Trese pulled up and parked. Vann hurried and called Darren to tell him what had just happened. But it really puzzled him that Chenelle knew Trese's name.

Vann heard Trese knock at the door. "Aight D. I'ma get at you later. That's baby girl at the door," Vann told Darren.

"Aight V. Oh yeah we going to see Greedy pretty soon, so be ready," Darren said.

"Yeah." Vann quickly hung up the phone. Trese knocked again and Vann quickly opened the door. Trese had a big smile on her face and Vann greeted her with a hug. It felt like they hadn't seen each other in a long time.

"Ummm…you smell good. Damn Girl! Why you do me like that? You know that's what I like. I can just taste you right now," Vann said to Trese while inhaling her sweet scented perfume. Vann closed the door.

"You like that, huh?" Trese asked him. She moved in closer to him. She wanted Vann real bad; probably as bad as he wanted her, but she knew that wasn't about to happen.

As she moved in closer to him, he grabbed her pulling her closer to him and then he kissed her softly on the lips and then aggressively on her neck. He knew Trese's neck was her spot and she got weak as soon as he made his move. It was like she couldn't resist him. She had to force herself away from him. Vann looked at Trese with a confused look on his face, like why did you do that.

"So, how you been baby?" she asked him.

"Oh, I've been good and how about you?" Vann asked her.

"I've been okay. I really need to talk to you about something. It's nothing major. I just want the truth," she told him. So they both

# Circles

went and sat down on the couch. Vann looked at Trese and Trese looked at him back with a sincere look on her face. "Have you been to the clinic recently baby?" she asked him.

Vann's facial expression changed quickly into disappointment. He just knew his girl couldn't have known about the situation he was in. "Yeah, why do you ask?" he asked her.

"Well, because I've been hearing about the whole Greedy thing and supposedly you were involved with the same girl… Chenelle." Trese continued and told him that her good friend Tremaine told her and his reason for telling her.

Vann couldn't believe what he was hearing. He shook his head and, afterwards, he couldn't even look Trese in the eyes because he was feeling guilty and shameful.

"Tremaine! Trese, who in tha fuck is Tremaine and how he know about me and what tha fuck I'm doing?!" Vann was raged to have even known that his woman was saying another guy's name that she was actually listening to.

"That doesn't matter Vann!" she yelled.

"Damn is that all you can think about is the drama, be concerned about me baby! About me almost getting infected with that shit and bringing it back to you! Did you think about that, huh?" he asked her.

Trese couldn't believe he went there with her, but he did. "So, you think I'm wrong for not asking you Vann? No, uh uh! You're the one who is wrong for even fucking around and then hiding the shit!" she yelled.

After Trese told him everything and after they shared their last words, she told him that she didn't think she could trust him anymore. Vann wasn't trying to argue with her, he just wanted her to understand where he was coming from. He knew that, when he heard those words, their relationship was falling apart and that was something he really didn't want to happen. Vann felt stupid because he knew he should have been up front with Trese, but he didn't because he was afraid of something like this happening. He knew he had failed Trese and he had to put something together to gain her trust back; and fast.

Trese left that night leaving the conversation they had with something to think about on both ends. She went over to Peaches' crib. Of course, Peaches was the one who told her everything. What kind of best friend would she have been had she not told Trese

# Heather Jornay Perkins

everything. Peaches got the information from Chase, her boyfriend. Trese really didn't want to leave Vann, but she knew it was the only way she could let him know that she was serious about the whole situation.

Vann laid on his bed, smelling the burning scented candles and the rose petals that were thrown across the bed. He laid there in silence visualizing the entire situation and what went wrong. He knew that he was wrong, but he thought that Trese would understand that he was only trying to keep her from getting hurt. Vann was trying to avoid what had just happened, them breaking up. He knew that he had made a mistake and he would do anything to do it all over again. Sleeping with Chenelle was the worst decision that he had ever made and especially when he knew Trese was a good woman to him, and possibly the one for him.

While Vann was moping and thinking, Trese kicked it with Peaches and Chase for a while, Chenelle was on her way back to Houston, Greedy was in the black hole because he had a major breakdown, Darren was with his baby mama Sonya, Gena was at home with her mother, Greedy's mother was at home with her grandbabies waiting to hear from Tracie, and Tremaine was in denial that he was one of the one's infected with the virus. They were all in this tremendous circle that was much deeper than it appeared. So much devastation had happened in such a short amount of time and so much was accounted for in so many small ways. Things didn't need to get any worst than it already was.

Tremaine recounted the countless times that he and Lace had sex; all those times that they never used protection. He was for sure breaking down and he needed someone to lean on. So he called Trese and they met up at the Red Bird Suites on Westmoreland in the Oakcliff. "Are you okay Tremaine?" Trese asked him.

Tremaine was laid back in the bed with one arm behind his head and he was biting his bottom lip. He usually did that when he had something on his mind. "Nah, nah. I'm aight," he answered.

"O...okay. Damn what's on this TV? You know when you first turn on these things they always have on a flick," she told him while laughing. Trese was trying to get Tremaine to smile or at least laugh a little, but he didn't.

"Say, come here." Tremaine had a lot on his mind and he was feeling needy and wanted to be loved.

Trese came and laid by him. He grabbed her with both of his

97

# Circles

hands, lifting her up, and placing her on top of him. They looked into each others eyes and Trese started smiling. Tremaine then leaned up and kissed her. They started kissing passionately which led to a night of love making. Trese really didn't want to make love to Tremaine; she only wanted to make love to Vann, but she was still upset with him and she had to get her orgasm some kind of way.

As time ticked away, and the night slipped by, Tremaine and Trese were nicely cuddled in each other's arms. They were exhausted from the love making that lasted nearly all night.

It was going on 9:37 a.m. and Gena was frustrated at the fact that she felt that there was no doubt that she was infected. While lying down on her bed, she closed her eyes and started thinking about all of the things that she and Greedy had been through. Gena couldn't believe how something like this happened so quickly.

Chase was there when the phone rang. He busted in Gena's room and handed her the phone. "Boy! Stop busting in my room like that!" Gena yelled.

Chase started laughing. "Here sis, it's the clinic," he said. Gena then placed her hand over her mouth; she was shocked that the clinic had called her back so soon.

"Hello," Gena said while holding the phone closely to her ear.

"Hi Gena this is Denise from the clinic. The reason why I am calling is to inform you that your results came back positive and the doctor would like for you to come back in as soon as you can. Do you know when you will be able to come back?" Denise asked her.

"Well...," Gena said.

"Can you come in this afternoon?" Denise asked Gena.

"Okay, I will be there," Gena told Denise. When she hung up, Gena gave Chase back the phone.

Quite naturally, Chase wanted to know exactly what the nurse said to her. "Gena what did she say?" Chase asked her.

Gena was spaced out when she answered, "That I'm positive and she told me to come in this afternoon."

"What?! Damn it Gena!" Chase said loudly. He was shocked. He said it so loudly that he woke their mother up in the next room. She came out the room to see what all the commotion was about. Gena's face just said it all. Her mother knew instantly what was going on so she sat by Gena on the bed.

"Baby, are you okay?" her mother asked her. Gena didn't say anything as tears rolled down her face. Her mother immediately comforted her and held her reassuring her that everything was going to be okay. But, there was no doubt in Gena's mind that she would soon be gone and it was all because she had unprotected sex; a mistake that wasn't even given any thought.

Gena hugged her mother back tightly and her brother walked out of the room. Chase had a lot of anger built up inside of him for so long about the hold thing. It really bothered him because that was his sister and nothing like this was supposed to be happening to her. Gena told her mother what the nurse told her, to be at the clinic. Gena's mother made it her first priority to be with her daughter and to get through this with her no matter what.

After Chase stormed out, he left headed towards Peaches' crib. Leaving with his windows rolled all the way down and his music playing extremely loud, he was frustrated and really disturbed. Chase couldn't believe his best friend Greedy did his sister the way he did. He loved Greedy like the older brother he never had. But, now things were going to be a lot different between them. Having Greedy in jail wasn't enough for him; he wanted Greedy to suffer.

Chase's phone rang and it was Gena calling him to see if he was okay. "Hey are you okay and where are you?" she asked him.

"Man sis. I can't handle shit like this, so I had to just take a drive. I'm on my way over to Peaches'. I need to think for a minute. Sis, don't worry about me. I'm good. You just get yourself together, okay," he told her.

"Chase you know I'm gunna do that. Mama is going with me okay and I will call you later and let you know what happened," Gena said.

"Aight," Chase said.

Chase finally made it over to Peaches. "Baby hit this so you can relax a bit. I know you're upset but things happen for a reason and some things we just can't change," Peaches told him. She kissed him on the lips and then gave him the blunt to fire up. Chase grabbed the blunt and sat back on the couch to unwind. Peaches, was really worried about Chase because he was really taking the news hard. So she did her best to make him feel more relaxed. Chase was so frustrated and angry, but he began to come to the realization that he really couldn't blame Greedy or his sister for their actions because, when it was all said and done, it was their decision to do whatever they chose. Chase started seeing the bigger picture about using protection. This was a serious issue and he now felt like safe sex

# Circles

should be taken into consideration at all times. Now his sister and his best friend were the ones in the mix.

"Gerald Reed. You have visitors at window nine. Window nine," the guard yelled through the intercom. One of the guards took Greedy to the window. When he approached the window he saw his mother, Darren, and Vann were his visitors. He was surprised because he didn't expect for anyone, not even his mother, to come and see him after what he did.

GREEDY SAT DOWN and then picked up the phone slowly. On the other side, his mother sat down and picked up the other phone. Vann and Darren stood behind her staring at Greedy like he killed someone, even though he really did. "Hey baby. Are you okay in here?" his mother asked him while trying to keep a smile on her face. She knew what Greedy had done but he was still her son and she had unconditional love for him.

"I'm okay mama. How about you? Are you okay?" he asked her.

"I'm doing just fine; just taking it one day at a time. You know you and your sister hit me hard this time and all I can do is ask God to take this hurt and pain away from me and to keep me strong." Greedy smiled. He really didn't have anything to say from what she said. He knew his mother was in a great deal of pain.

"Have you heard from Tracie yet?" Greedy asked her.

"Yes, I've spoken to her and she said that she really hated to hear about you and what you were going through. She wants you to give yourself to the Lord and try and get past this. She wants to hear from you so please write her, okay," she told him.

Ms. G was glad to see her son, but she still had a lot of things on her mind. He told his mother that he was supposed to be coming up for trial and he would let her know as soon as he got more information.

"You know Gerald, I love you very much and I want you to stay strong for me in there and do what you know is best," she told him. Greedy told his mother that he loved her and after she finished talking to him she handed the phone to Darren. He knew his mother was heartbroken and he really couldn't face her the way he would have liked to knowing that he brought most of the pain.

While hanging his head down, Darren grabbed the phone

and Vann stepped forward. Darren wanted to talk to Greedy first. Greedy looked up at Darren with disappointment. "Say G, we didn't come down here to preach to ya. You still our boy and you know we wouldn't have come down here if we didn't care about you. I know you bro and I can't be the one to blame you," Darren told him.

"I know and I can't blame you, Vann, Chase, or whoever for the way you may think of me. I mean, I wish I could take everything back; but this shit is so fucked up, dawg, that I had to do something and do something to someone for doing it to me," Greedy told him with no hesitation.

"Yeah man we gunna miss you out here. I'ma let you talk to V aight. Love you boy," Darren told Greedy while passing the phone to Vann.

"Wassup nigga!" Vann said.

"Wassup," Greedy answered.

"You know I'ma say what's on my mind. Shit you know that shit was fucked up about the way you did things. Yeah, you did that and it's over with; but damn Greedy, you killed Lace my nigga!" Vann said to Greedy with anger.

"Man! You have no idea what tha fuck is going on with me and how the fuck I feel!" Greedy told him.

"Yeah, I know you've changed nigga! I see things are different now," Vann said. Vann had so much anger towards Greedy. He felt like there was no excuse for what Greedy did.

Greedy laughed it off and then looked at Vann straight in the face. "I knew you were going to be the one to not hold back and I can respect that. But V, this bitch turned around and gave me the shit bro and this eventually is going to lead to full blown AIDS if I don't get treated and you know that shit ain't right! I mean, what did I do to deserve this. Now my future is fucked up!" Greedy was so upset that tears started to fall down his face.

Vann felt no sympathy for Greedy. He stood up and started lashing out on Greedy like it was nothing. "Man nigga you are the one who decided to fuck up! Instead of finding out who gave it to you, you just picked out who did. Then nigga you didn't even go and get checked out. You just blamed your girl. That was fucked up G! You know this!" Vann started hitting on the glass, yelling at Greedy for all the wrong he had done and the damage he caused.

The guards immediately stopped the visitation. Darren grabbed Vann and the guards escorted them all downstairs and the

# Circles

guard took Greedy back to his cell. On the way back from the jail, everyone was quiet, there was absolutely no conversation. There was nothing to discuss after what just happened. Vann was still heated, Darren was disappointed, and Ms. G was still shocked to know that her son had killed an innocent woman and was infected with the HIV virus.

Heather Jornay Perkins

Circles


## 10. PICKING UP THE PIECES


THE AFTERNOON WAS almost over and Gena and her mother were finishing up at the clinic and Chase was still over at Peaches' house. When Gena and her mother made it back she called Chase and asked him to come home so she could fill him in with what the doctor told her. When Chase left Peaches', she called Trese to see if she was okay and where she was.

Trese's phone didn't even ring. It went straight to voicemail. Anytime Trese had her phone calls going straight to voicemail, it was because she was at work or busy. Peaches had forgotten that Trese had a Job Fair to present at that afternoon, so she assumed that Trese was still with Tremaine. Peaches left her a message telling her to call her back.

While Trese was at work, she received a text message, from Vann, that read: Baby, we need to talk. We can't keep avoiding each other like this. I can't stand it when we are mad at each other. So whenever you're ready I'm here.

After Trese read the text message, she realized that deep down inside she knew he was sincerely sorry and she really did miss him. In her heart, she missed him; but in her mind, she couldn't get over what he had done.

Trese walked to the break room to call Vann, but when she placed her hand on the phone, she pulled away. She felt lost for words and she had a lot on her mind although she knew Vann was right, they did need to talk.

After Vann sent his text message to Trese, he prayed that she would have at least called or texted him back but she didn't; at least not as quickly as he wanted her to. He hopped in the shower, the place where he could go when he needed to relax and think. He contemplated on how he was going to get his baby girl back or if it was too late.

Trese knew what she had to do with Vann, but after

kicking it with Tremaine the other night, her situation became a lot harder. While she was in the break room she turned her phone back on to accept phone calls. She noticed that she had a voice message. It was her best friend Peaches saying to call her. Trese waited before calling her back until she finished up at work.

While things were a little tense around Trese, they were just dying down with Gena. Chase came in and walked straight to the bathroom, passing Gena and their mother. He had to go real bad. When he came back out, he went to the front and sat next to Gena. "So, what happened sis?" he asked her.

"All I can say right now is that I will be fine as long as I'm treated, and the doctor keeps saying that everything will be ok," she told him.

Chase was still skeptical because his sister still looked down and out in the dumps. He couldn't help but to ask what else was bothering her. So Gena told him that she wanted to see Greedy because she needed some closure between them. Chase couldn't disagree with her because he knew how his sister felt about Greedy and they both had been through a lot with each other. Gena wanted to talk to Greedy and see him for one last time. She felt the need to ask him again, face-to-face, why did this have to happen to her and he was the only one who could satisfy her with a response.

Gena left the living room, went to her bedroom, and started to write Greedy a letter to let him know that she would be down there to see him real soon. Deep down, Gena still loved Greedy. It never seemed to amaze her how he always found a way to mess their relationship up. But at this point, there wasn't anything else that could mess up what was already destroyed.

The evening went and the nighttime came, and that's when Trese finally gave Vann a call. Vann was lying on his bed when his phone suddenly rang. He looked and saw that it was Trese calling him. Vann hurried and picked up the phone, not trying to sound like he was actually waiting on her to call him; nevertheless, he had been anxiously waiting all day.

"Hey," Trese said.

"Yeah, wassup?" Vann asked her.

"Well, I read your text message and I know I've been

avoiding you and we both been going through some things. I agree with that. We both need to sit down and talk. I mean we still have a lot to discuss," Trese told him.

"So, you want to talk now, or are you busy?" he asked her.

"No, I'm not busy. I called you because I thought maybe you would want to talk about this now too," she told him.

Vann began to smile. "Okay. So do you want to meet up or are you coming over?" he asked her.

"I will be over there," Trese said while laughing a little. After she hung up with Vann, she tried calling Peaches but her line kept ringing busy. She wanted to let Peaches know that she was on her way to sit and talk with Vann but, since her phone stayed continuously busy, that information would have to be conveyed to Peaches after the fact.

Trese went ahead and took a shower and slipped into something more comfortable. By the time she sat down to put lotion on her legs, she heard a knock at her door. When she opened the door, it was Vann. Trese didn't say anything as she was surprised to see him. She only responded with a smile.

She let him in and he gave her a hug; the kind of hug which let her know that he needed her. Trese knew that he missed her a lot and she hugged him back even tighter and longer than usual, inhaling his cologne scent. After the long hugging, they both went in her room and sat down on her bed. Trese asked him if he wanted anything to drink. He answered yes so she went to the kitchen and brought back sodas for both of them.

She placed the drinks on the nightstand next to her bed and sat down right beside Vann. "So, why couldn't you tell me what was up with you V?" she asked him.

"What exactly are you asking me? What do you want to know?" Vann asked her.

"First, I need to know why you didn't mention anything about Greedy to me; the whole HIV thing and him killing that stripper girl?" Trese asked.

"Greedy…HIV," Vann mumbled in a low tone.

"Yes Greedy and that girl! That's some straight up bullshit for you to keep that from me!" Trese exclaimed.

"I know. I know baby. I just didn't want to upset you and for you to worry about me and my boys," Vann told her.

"Worry…and that's what I'm supposed to do. Be concerned for you Vann. I'm glad you went and got checked out. I know you didn't really want to discuss Chenelle, but I do because that issue is on my mind too! I know you and Chenelle had a thing before I came around, so you should've had enough trust in me to tell me everything." Trese then grabbed Vann's face and started speaking in a soft tone, "Baby I care about you so much and I love you. But you do some crazy things and I can't figure you out sometimes."

Vann looked at Trese in her eyes and smiled. "Dang Trese! Baby so you really do love me? I mean, you sound so sincere," he said softly back to her.

"Oh. I know how much I say it, and I show it a lot. But yes, really baby, I do. I really do," she gently replied.

"Man, just hearing you say those words makes me feel so much more for you," Vann said.

"Before you say anything else I..." As Trese was about to ask Vann an important question, her cell phone started to ring interrupting their intimate conversation.

It was Peaches again so Trese answered the phone. Hey girl, wassup?" Trese asked her.

"Girl, we need to talk and this really can't wait," Peaches said.

"Peaches it's gunna have to wait, okay. Don't worry I will call you as soon as I finish," Trese told her.

"Okay," Peaches said before she hung up. Trese wasn't really trying to hear what Peaches was talking about right then anyway. She had something more important going on and it really couldn't wait. Trese's mind was all focused on her and Vann getting back together.

"Ole Peaches still blowing you up huh?" Vann asked.

"Uh huh. Like always. But anyway. I did want to ask you something, but it can wait. All I want to do right now is hold you," Trese said. She made that clear because she really wanted Vann to know that she really did miss him just as much as he missed her.

"Oh yeah," he said. Vann pushed up closely to Trese and kissed her neck inhaling her sweet fragrance. He slowly

# Circles

rubbed her back while Trese was embraced with just his touch alone. "You know I thought we were through for a minute there, even though I wasn't ready to just accept it at that. Damn, I've been missing you girl!" he told Trese. He kissed up and down her neck and then down to her chest where her nipples were perky from the excitement she was feeling for Vann. Trese's plan wasn't to have sex with Vann, but he was so aggressive that he made her feel like she would have been missing out on a good thing if she didn't. So she gave in and they had passionate make up sex. Usually they used protection, but this time they didn't because Trese told Vann that she wanted to feel him; and feeling him is exactly what she got. It was the best sex Trese and Vann had ever experienced with each other.

After the making up was over, Trese and Vann fell asleep in each other's arms. Trese put her phone on silent so she wouldn't be disturbed by anyone. Trese had a message from Tremaine. He had called her earlier but she forgot to call him back. Trese call me. I really need to talk to you about something, so hit me up aight. Tremaine couldn't believe the news he heard about Lace and now he really had a lot on his mind, including the fact that he had to share this information with the person he truly loved. He had falling in love with Trese, but Trese was in love with someone else.

Trese had a lot to sort through herself because she was playing with two people and their feelings. She liked Tremaine and loved him as a friend; but she had never thought of him as being the one for her, that is until recently when she started entertaining the idea. Trese was clueless and confused.

The next day came and Darren was over at Greedy's mother's house. "Thank you Darren for being a supportive friend to Greedy. He really needs us and he really appreciates everything you've been doing for him and his family besides just being mad at him." Greedy's mother had so much respect for Darren. She thought it was very loyal of him to do the things that he had done recently.

"You're welcome Ms. G. Anytime," Darren told her. Darren had come over to Greedy's mother's crib to drop off some money for her, the kids, and for Greedy and his sister while they were locked up. Ms. G was so happy that Darren was helping her out because times were rough for her at that time.

After stopping by Greedy's mother's house, Darren headed towards Trese's crib. Vann was still sleeping wrapped under Trese. Darren didn't even call Vann to let him know that he was on his way.

"Ummm, baby you want some breakfast?" Trese asked Vann as she began to rise from her restful sleep.

"Whatever you cook baby, you know I'm all for it," Vann told her.

"Oh really? So if I bring you a can of worms, will you eat them?" Trese asked him trying to be funny.

"Man girl! You know what I'm saying. But I tell you what, I would eat them for you though," Vann said. She started blushing and then turned around and kissed him softly.

Back at Trese place, Darren honked his horn while sitting in front of her apartment. Vann looked out and saw that it was Darren. "Damn! I forgot this nigga was coming here over to scoop me up. I told him that I was going to be at your crib and he remembered," Vann said out loud.

"For what? Where are ya'll going?" Trese asked while trying to hurry and slip on something decent.

"We have some business to take care of and then go by and check on Chase," he told her.

"Ohhhh, business. Okay," Trese said.


AFTER TRESE FINISHED slipping something on, she walked up behind Vann and embraced him with a hug and a kiss on his back. He grabbed her hands and kissed them gently. While they fooled around in the room, playing like some little kids, Darren became impatient with the no response he was receiving from Vann so he got out his car and walked to the door and knocked. He didn't get an answer, so he knocked even harder. Vann came and opened the door. "Damn nigga!" Darren said as soon as Vann let him in. Vann couldn't do anything, but smile.

"What's up boy!" Vann slapped hands with Darren.

Trese came out the bedroom. "Hey, what's up D?" she asked Darren.

Darren was speechless. After all Vann and Trese had been through, he didn't expect for him to still be with her and spending the night over at her apartment; but he did. He didn't really know what to say to her, "Nothing much, what's good with ya?" he asked her.

"Oh nothin much," she told him with a little smirk on her face.

Vann was on his way out the door. It was now no point in Trese cooking breakfast for him. As she started to walk Vann to the door, she grabbed Vann's hands and pulled him back towards the door. She kissed him on the cheek and then told him that she would see him later. "Aight baby, I'll see you later. Be good," Darren told her while walking out the door.

After Trese let Vann and Darren out, Darren couldn't wait to ask Vann if they were back together. Vann could tell when Darren wanted to know something because he would always have this crazy look on his face that said everything his mouth wanted to say. "Man! Don't even ask cuz you already know bro," Vann told him before he could even get started.

Darren started laughing. "Ask you what bro? What you talking about?" Vann looked at Darren like man don't play stupid. "Oh man. I knew that was bound to happen. I knew that shit," Darren said.

"Yeah, whatever man. So you talked to that nigga Chase?" Vann asked Darren as he walked back to the room to get dressed.

"Nope. That nigga still been trippin' since he found out that shit about his sister," Darren said.

Trese called Peaches back. "Damn bitch! I've been trying to call you and text you because I had something else to tell you. And this time it's about Tremaine!" Peaches didn't sound too happy.

"What?" Trese asked.

"Okay. Did he tell you that he had not too long ago just been with that stripper hoe Lace; that stripper girl Greedy killed? The whole time he has been messing around with you!" Peaches exclaimed.

"No, he didn't tell me that! He said that he use to kick it with her a while back…I know this nigga didn't just lie about that shit!" Trese said.

"Damn! So that nigga is dirty fo' real and that's not good Trese," Peaches told her.

"I know. Fuck! Hell nah fuck this shit!" Trese screamed.

She hung up in Peaches' face. Trese didn't mean to hang up on Peaches like that, but she was hysterical and needed to get a hold of Tremaine. Trese tried calling Tremaine on his cell, but she didn't get an answer. She didn't want to leave him a message. She needed to have a live conversation with his ass.

Trese was so desperate to talk to him that she turned around and headed towards where she knew he always hung out over in South Dallas off Stoneman and Leland. Trese was pissed off but still prayed to God that neither she nor Tremaine were infected.

She pulled up on Stoneman Street and got out of the car. She didn't know precisely where Tremaine hung out at so she just yelled his name a few times to see if he would come out or if anyone would tell her where he was. People were staring at her like she was a crazy clucker off the street.

Tremaine heard her. He was in the red and white house on the corner. When he came out he had this slick grin on his face. "Wassup baby and why tha fuck are you out here yelling?" he asked her. But Trese wasn't fucking around with him. She slapped him so hard that that grin came right off of his face. Tremaine had to control his reaction because she hit him so hard that he could have hit her back.

"Bitch are you crazy?! What tha fuck was that for?" Tremaine asked Trese while rubbing the left side of his face. Tremaine grabbed her and pulled her towards her car. They both got in and that's when things got heated up more. Trese calmed down and began to question him.

"Did you ever have sex with Lace? And was it recently?" Tremaine's answer had to be simple. It was either yes or no.

"Yes I did a few times. But that doesn't mean anything," he said.

"Okay. Well, did you know that she was HIV positive and did you even bother to use protection with her? Be honest Tremaine because this is some serious shit," she told him trying to fight back the tears.

"Yes I used protection with her!" he said.

All of a sudden, Trese started crying and hitting Tremaine in the arm. "What the fuck Tremaine! I know you didn't always use protection with her! You're not telling me the truth!" Trese said.

"Damn! Okay baby. Trese I did have unprotected sex with her once, but that doesn't mean that I'm infected; and neither are you! I know we're not infected with HIV!" Tremaine told her trying to calm her down.

Trese wiped her tears and sniffled a little. "So, you don't even know if you are or not? When was the last time you got tested? Huh?!" she asked him. Trese was upset and angry beyond belief and she demanded answers. The first thing that came to her mind was how she was going to tell Vann, the person who she truly loved and had been cheating on all this time. It was the same as Vann not telling her that he slept with Chenelle recently. All Trese had was that Chenelle was an old piece of game that Vann was once involved with. Trese had no idea that Vann had just gone through the same thing with Chenelle.

After having their conversation, Tremaine knew he couldn't make anymore assumptions. He had to get tested and Trese did too. He got out of the car and Trese burnt off quickly. She was so mad that she didn't even say goodbye. Trese was a total wreck. It would have been impossible for her to have a good day at work so she called in. That was something that Trese never did. She didn't know how she was going to break the news to Vann. Honestly she wasn't even sure if she could be a real woman about the whole situation and tell him at all. But, she didn't want to keep this from him because, if she did, she wouldn't be able to live with herself knowing that she covered up something of this magnitude. Trese didn't know which part was going to hurt him the worst; the cheating or that she could possibly be infected with the HIV virus.

Heather Jornay Perkins

Circles

## 11. ONE TIME, TWO, TOO MANY

PEACHES AND CHASE were on their way out the door when
Trese pulled up. She got out of the car and told Peaches that she
needed to talk to her alone. So, Chase went on and got in the
car and Peaches and Trese went inside the house. Peaches knew
that Trese had been crying because her eyes were puffy. Trese
told Peaches everything that she and Tremaine talked about.
Peaches knew that her friend was seriously hurting and she
knew Trese wasn't gone be able to handle it alone. Trese cried
and cried and Peaches couldn't do anything but hold her and
give her the love and support that a best friend could give.
 Like anyone else in this situation, Trese didn't know
what to expect. Would things get worst or would things get
better? And in this case, how much better? Peaches told Trese
that she needed to go and get herself checked out and that she
would call her once she made it to work. Trese couldn't face
anyone else, besides Peaches, right now; not even her father.
She couldn't believe how things could change so quickly. What
she didn't know was that many things had changed. Not only
for her, but for a lot of people since the whole HIV issue began.
Since the incident with Greedy, it seemed as though everything
and everyone was falling apart.
 Meanwhile, Gena was finally on her way to see Greedy,
unsure of how she was going to feel when she saw him. She still
held to the truth of, even though she had unresolved issues
with Greedy, she still loved him so much that words couldn't
explain it.
 When she arrived, Gena took a seat in front of window
seven. She was more nervous than calm. She hadn't seen
Greedy in months now. She really needed to see him and talk
to him because the words on paper really couldn't express what

was really going on between them. Greedy approached
the window and smiled when he seen that Gena was the one
visiting him. In the back of his mind, he never thought that
Gena would be the person to come and see him after all he'd
put her through. Greedy loved Gena so much that even if she
hated him, he'd still love her forever.

When they both picked up the phones, there was
about five seconds of complete silence. Then Gena started the
conversation. "Hey. So how are you?" she asked.

"Hey to you too. I've been okay. Just hanging in there,"
he told her. Gena placed her hand on the window, but Greedy
was too stubborn because he was trying to avoid showing any
emotion. But he had to let the stubbornness go. It was
impossible for him to do anymore harm to Gena so he placed
his hand on the glass making it appear as though they were
touching hands through the glass.

"Gena, before you say anything let me go first okay,"
Greedy told her.

"Okay," she said while smiling. Gena had tears in her
eyes but she tried with all of her might to hold it because she
knew it would only make it harder for Greedy while he was
locked up.

"I want you to know that I'm sorry and I mean it
from the bottom of my heart. I truly apologize for putting you
through this madness. You shouldn't be going through this. You
are a good person. Baby, I never meant to hurt you and I surely
didn't intend on anything like this to happen to us. You're my
girl and I still love you so damn much. I can only ask that you
forgive me and not for your sympathy. Can you accept what has
happened and forgive me please?" Greedy didn't know what
else to say. All he knew was that he was sorry for everything
and that he didn't want Gena to hold any grudges against him.

Gena was stunned that he asked her for forgiveness,
including everything else he said. "I do forgive you and as far
as accepting the situation, that's already done. I have no choice.
But, I'm curious about something and I need you to be honest
with me Greedy," Gena said.

"Okay, what?" Greedy asked.

"Do you know if Lace was really the one who gave
you HIV? Are you really sure about that? Or was it possibly

someone else?" she asked him. Greedy looked at Gena with the most disturbing look on his face. He couldn't believe Gena was playing detective now that she outwardly didn't trust him.

Something that was never discussed ran through Greedy's mind and, before Gena knew it, Greedy stood up and cursed her out about not trusting in him. He threw the chair against the window and then the guard rushed to get Greedy and take him back to his cell. He never answered Gena's question, yet it was obvious that something else was bothering him.

Gena slowly placed the phone back on the hook while still staring in at the emptiness on the other side of the glass. Her mind was boggled up with thoughts; thoughts that she couldn't possibly get rid of. She stood up and walked off as the others, visiting their loved ones, watched her pass by.

She walked back to her car and sat inside for a while before driving away. What else was Greedy hiding and why did it make him so angry at her? Gena couldn't put her finger on it, she was clueless. But she knew that whatever it was, she would soon find out.

On the other side of town, Darren, Vann, and Chase met up and headed towards the drag racing track, Yellow Belly. The track was always krunk; especially on Sundays. Being out there was like being at a club's parking lot. All of the guys were G'd up and all the ladies were flossed to perfection. But the main attractions were the races and the bets placed on them. "Man, I haven't been out here in a minute!" Darren shouted.

"Yeah. Me neither," Chase said while holding his beer in his left hand and a blunt in his right. Chase was there at the track, but his mind wasn't.

"Now see little bro, this is the kind of shit that gets your mind off the other things," Vann told Chase.

"Yeah, man. I know you been stressing lately, but today is the day for you to relax and enjoy yourself a little. You know what I'm saying bro?" Darren asked him.

"Yeah, I hear you and I hear you too Vann. Y'all right. I have been tripping lately since the shit hit the fan, but I'm glad I have you both. You might as well say we're like brothers and I appreciate what y'all trying to do. Today is the day to kick it, huh?!" Chase agreed with them.

"Already, my nigga, already," Vann said while slapping hands with him and giving him a brotherly hug.

Chase, Vann, and Darren chilled and kicked it at the track a little while longer. Chase was trying to enjoy himself to avoid thinking about his sister. To him, nothing could get any worse than his sister's situation.

Gena knew what she was up against, but she still wanted to really know why Greedy got so hostile with her. She started her investigation with being nosey and going around and asking, the people Greedy hung around with, questions. But, regretfully, she came up with no answers. This did not discourage Gena though. She was determined to find out the truth, the whole truth, and nothing but the truth.

While back in his cell, Greedy felt bad about his reaction towards Gena. He knew he was wrong but he had wronged her in so many ways, he didn't know where to start with telling the truth. He had so many things built up inside of him that he really wanted to pour out to Gena. There was no perfect way to start so Greedy decided that he was ready to start fessing up Gena, so he decided to write her a letter so he could let her know what was really going on with him; the things she didn't know.

*Gena,*

*You are the one and only woman I've ever had true feelings for and loved. You asked me an important question and I really didn't know how to respond to you. So, I flipped and I know I shouldn't have because you deserve to know about what's been going on with me. The truth, the honest truth I really can't say if it was Lace or not who gave me this, but I knew that we did sleep together a few times and no there was no protection used. She wasn't the only person that I've slept with unprotected and that I could have gotten it from. Well, now I know your thinking damn! I know, but this is the truth and besides I know you weren't faithful to me as you say you were either...*

*G*

GENA RECEIVED GREEDY'S letter in the mail on June 6. After she read it, she took the information for what it was. She

# Circles

couldn't believe Greedy and the mess he had put her through and then had the nerve to talk about love. Gena didn't write back or accept anymore of his calls. And she did not go back to see him. She finally realized that it was time to face it and just to leave him alone and do for herself. So that's exactly what she did. Gena took the letter that she received from Greedy and made copies of it and gave it to a lot of people to read. She wanted to see if someone would come forward about who truly gave him HIV.

Everyone was in total shock about the letter except for Six. When Six was given the letter by Gena, he didn't know what to expect. After he read it, he looked at Gena and then asked her was that all of the information that Greedy had given her. Gena looked at him like why would you ask me something like that.

"No, no he didn't." Gena was wondering why Six would think Greedy had told her something else.

"Oh, okay. I was just wondering because the letter sounded so bland." Six didn't say anything else after that. Six then led Gena towards the door and he opened the door, politely showing her the way out. He wasn't trying to be rude with her, but he was. He was really upset with Greedy and trying to hide the fact that they were intimate once upon a time.

As soon as Gena stepped out the door and turned around to say something else, Six shut the door in her face. Gena found herself standing and facing a closed door remembering how Tracie, Keeno, Jewell, Tank, Six, and Greedy use to hit check licks together.

Gena knocked back on his door. Six didn't want to be mean to her so he let her in and, right then and there, she knew she was close to what Greedy was hiding. Gena wanted to talk to someone and she really wanted Six to listen to her. Gena started talking about what she and Greedy had been through and how he kept hiding things from her. She even went so far as to discuss the entire ordeal about HIV and how it was taking her through a storm. When she mentioned the virus, Six's eyes widened. He began acting a little nervous like something was bothering him.

After she told him that Greedy had given her the virus

he acted like he was in total shock about the whole situation.

"I can't believe him…I really can't," Six told her being a little flamboyant. Gena looked at Six and, by the way he was looking into her eyes, you could tell that he was also hurt. Six tried to not show it but he was too emotional not to. He started fanning his face with his hands trying to avoid the tears that were welling up. "Oh, I'm trying not to cry because this shit doesn't make any sense Gena!" Six said while tears finally started to roll down his face. Gena didn't know if Six was hurt by what Greedy did to her or by what someone had done to him.

Gena had an awkward look on her face. When Six glanced at Gena, he noticed how she was looking at him funny. He wiped his tears and rushed Gena by asking her if she would come back because he was a bit too emotional and needed sometime to himself. At that moment, Gena knew that something must have happened between the two of them.

As she was about to walk out of the door, she stopped, turned around, and touched Six on his shoulder. "Six, I don't know what happened between you and Greedy, or why it happened for that matter, but I am so upset with Greedy's words that I can't even explain it. My heart is in so much pain right now that only God can help me in this situation. But as for you, it sounds like you are hurt and whatever you and Greedy had going on that's none of my business. The only thing I ask is that you go get tested and whoever else you think might possibly have it." After saying that to Six, Gena walked away feeling much more relieved than she did before she walked in. Six was shocked to hear her talk like that especially finding out something about someone she truly cared about. Six felt like he shouldn't have taken the steps that he did to hurt Greedy the way he did. And now he knew what he had to do and why he had to do it.

Circles

## 12. THE VISIT

SIX PAID A visit to Greedy the next day. Greedy wasn't
expecting anyone else to come and visit him so when he heard
that he had a visitor he assumed it was his mother or Darren
coming to visit. The guard opened the door and the look on
Greedy's face turned into a look of confusion, and then he
frowned. Six had his legs crossed and his eyes were glued to
Greedy's. Greedy picked up the phone as he stared at Six
wondering why he came down to see him.

"Wassup?" Greedy asked.

"Don't look too thrilled to see me, do you?" Six asked
him.

"Hmm. Thrilled. I'm not going there with you Six. So
why did you come down here?" Greedy asked him.

"I've been hearing about you lately and I can't say I
don't understand why you did the things that you did because I
do. But there's one thing that I don't know," Six said.

"Don't know what?" Greedy asked.

"How did you know that Lace was the one who gave
you the virus?" Six asked him.

"Gave me what?!" Greedy had gotten upset because he
knew where the conversation was going. Six then whispered
into the phone, "You know the HIV..."

"Oh, so you think someone else gave it to me nigga?!"
Greedy asked. Greedy acted like he wanted to come through
the glass on Six.

"Let's say the night we were together, we didn't use
protection. And you were so into me that you never even
suggested it," Six told Greedy.

"Man, fuck you! You are a hoe ass nigga for that shit!
Man, fuck you! I wish I could kill your bitch ass! Punk ass
nigga!" Greedy was yelling and hitting the window very hard,

120

trying to break it. The guards had to take Greedy away again. He was clowning and Six didn't care because his loose ends with Greedy were finally finished; over with, done. Six knew what he did was wrong, but he wanted to get Greedy back for taking money from his safe a while back. That was back when they were in the check biz. Greedy didn't actually do it himself, but he had some ratchy niggas from the N.O. to do it for him for little to nothing. Six was hemmed up and Greedy was responsible for it.

One day Greedy walked in on Six putting some more money into his safe. It was over 50,000 dollars. When Greedy saw that, that's when he got the New Orleans niggas to jack Six. All that Six had was stolen just like that. From that point on, revenge was the only thing on Six's mind so the game plan was on. Six had a plan and he went through with it.

While time was ticking, the secrets and the things that were not told were now being unfolded. Six was really a friend of Greedy's a few years back before all of the drama hit. Everyone had a part in the check biz, but Six was the one with the major money. He had a lot of respect from a lot of people.

One night, Greedy was high off that wet and he had been stressing out about his money. He knew Six was the right person to talk about his situation and he knew Six would help him, even though he had some people to jack him for all that he had. Returning to the scene of the crime was what criminals and plotters did, like nothing ever happened. After Greedy told Six that he had owed this big time dope dealer named Cool C some money, Six offered to drive Greedy home because Greedy was in no shape to be driving himself. But, Greedy refused and decided to crash at Six's pad for the night, or until the drugs wore off. So, everything seemed cool. Six went back to his room and Greedy was stretched out on the couch.

While he was lying down, Six eased his way back into the living room. You see, Six was bi-sexual. He loved women and men. He slightly pulled Greedy's shirt up and kissed him on his stomach and then started to go down on him. Greedy didn't stop Six, he accepted the pleasure. Greedy was so desperate for money that he would have done anything to get it. Yes, he was that desperate. Six constantly stroked Greedy over and over and over making him forget all about his worries.

# Circles

After going down on Greedy, Greedy jumped up like what had he done. Knowing that he had crossed the line, Greedy looked at Six with the most crazy look. Six couldn't tell if the facial expression was good or bad. Greedy didn't say anything because to him, deep down inside, Six felt kind of good to him. Plus Greedy was still in a high mode and he really didn't care from that point on because he already knew that he had made a big mistake and there was no turning back now. Six felt so good to him that he continued with the intimate moment with him. Six went back down on Greedy, stroking and stroking him. Gently he grabbed his dick and held it in his hand stroking him harder and harder until Greedy nutted. "Damn, Fuck," Greedy moaned.

Six wanted more from Greedy that night. He wanted to get fucked and that's exactly what happened between them. Greedy had never had an experience with a man before neither had he ever given it to someone else in the ass. When Greedy nutted, Six knew he had to get him back on hard so he rubbed his dick and then placed Greedy's hand on his. After he stroked and stroked, he was like "Damn! This shit feels too damn good. Fuck!" as he came quickly with the most extreme urge of excitement. Six enjoyed every moment of it and didn't regret any of it.

After that, Greedy questioned himself as to whether or not he was now gay or bisexual, or had he just had a memorable experience. He also prayed that Six never told anybody about them. Now that Greedy was locked up and had received a visit by Six, Greedy couldn't help but to write Gena again and, this time, give her every detail of the truth, which is what she desired the most. Letting the truth be told by him instead of Six would help him get the pain and hurt off of his chest.

Gena couldn't believe that Greedy was actually telling her the truth even though she kind of figured things out after her visit with Six; and not to mention that she followed Six down to the jail when he visited Greedy. She read the letter twice because she couldn't believe he actually did something like this. She was hurt by the truth and even more devastated because not only did he have the HIV virus, he was gay! She wanted to tell someone but she couldn't. It was too harsh to let anyone else know about what happened.

Six knew he had to move because he didn't know if Gena had figured things out or not. He didn't want to take any more chances with another person popping up at his door uninvited.

After Six completed his revenge on Greedy, he went back to his place where his bags and all of his belongings were packed up and ready to go. He knew it was time for him to move back home to Atlanta. He knew staying in Dallas would bring more trouble for him especially if everyone found out about him and Greedy.

As for Greedy, he was relieved that he had got the pain and hurt off his chest. His mother and Darren kept coming to visit him and he wrote his sister Tracie and told her everything that had happened with him. Vann stopped going to visit Greedy and Chase visited every once in a while, but he did write. Gena never responded to the letter and continued to not go back down to visit him.

## 13. FACING THE TRUTH

AFTER TALKING TO Trese, Peaches jumped in the car with Chase and he drove her to work. Trese sat in her car for a few minutes before she pulled off. She felt devastated and very uncomfortable. All she wanted to do was get her situation resolved and fast. She didn't want any rumors to start or for Vann to find out in the wrong way. Trese started thinking about how he would react to such devastating news. She knew it would be the end for her and their relationship. Most of all, Vann would hate her forever.

It was Friday and Trese didn't want to waste anymore time. She immediately went to see Dr. Velez at Planned Parenthood. As soon as Trese arrived, time was ticking and the clinic was closing in thirty minutes. Trese had no more time to waste. She tried to stay calm, but her tears just wouldn't stop.

"Hi, do you have an appointment with us today?" the receptionist asked Trese.

While wiping her tears, Trese answered, "Um, nope. I need to see Dr. Velez." The receptionist noticed how upset Trese was and told her to have a seat while she went to go and get Dr. Velez for her. Trese sat down and, as she waited, her phone vibrated with an incoming call. It was Vann. She wanted to answer, but she knew it wasn't the right time to talk to him. Not until she had answers.

"Trese," Dr. Velez called her name after she opened the door. Trese stood up and followed her to one of the back rooms. "So, why the tears Trese? What's going on with you today?" Dr. Velez asked her as she held on to Trese medical chart.

"Well, I know that you have been educating me about using protection and it's just that right now, I would like to get tested for everything, including HIV." Trese cleared up her tears and spoke in an angry tone.

"Trese…," Dr. Velez didn't say another word. She just went over and held Trese tightly because she knew being in the position that she was in was really worst than she could have imagined. Dr. Velez reassured Trese that everything would be okay if the results came out positive or not. But, that wasn't enough for Trese. She crumbled and broke down in tears because she knew that she had gotten herself into something that she couldn't get out of.

Dr. Velez immediately ran all tests on her. After the testing, everything was a go except for the HIV test. The nurse told Trese that her results would be back within three business days. That made Trese feel worse than she was already feeling. The waiting period was going to drive her insane because she really didn't want to be around Vann until everything was in the clear. Vann meant the world to her and she didn't want to lose him.

On her way home, she listened to Mary J Blige and Usher's song, Shakedown. It was the holiday season; time to be with loved ones and here it was that so many things were going on in Trese's life. The year had gone by fast and it was ending in a worst way.

After making it home, Trese was very exhausted from all of the drama she was involved in. She took a nap and turned her phone completely off. She needed to be by herself at the moment. She was very depressed and her emotions were on a rollercoaster ride. While, Trese was taking her nap, of course, Vann tried calling her again and again, but there was no answer. So, he decided to stop by her place after he finished up at work.

While driving to Trese's place, Vann called Darren and asked him what was up for the weekend and reminded him that the holidays were coming up. "So, are you going to take Trese to meet your moms this Thanksgiving? You know moms has to meet her!" Darren asked him.

"Yeah, I was thinking about it and I will as soon as I tell my mother about her," Vann said and then started laughing. After Vann hung up with Darren, he was pulling up in Trese's apartments. Pulling up in front of her apartment complex, he parked and then headed towards her door.

# Circles

Trese was sound asleep and Vann tried to reach her again, but there was still no answer. Vann had a key to her place so he unlocked the door and went right on in. He closed the door silently and then locked it as quietly as he could. Vann placed his keys on the table and then slid his shoes off. As he peeked into Trese bedroom, he saw that she was asleep. "Damn, my baby must be tired," he said to himself. Vann slowly got into the bed and laid down behind her, wrapping his arms around her tightly.

"Mmmm," Trese sighed while grabbing Vann's hands tightly. Then she smiled and all of a sudden she opened her eyes and then jumped up.

"Vann!" she shouted.

"Yeah, baby, it's me," he said while giggling. He thought it was funny that Trese jumped up the way she did.

"I'm sorry baby. I forgot you had a spare key," she told him.

"Yeah, I see. Come here," he told her.

"Um. Okay," Trese said while getting back in the bed. Vann then kissed Trese behind the neck and then massaged her shoulders to the middle of her back.

"Ummm," she moaned. Trese couldn't resist Vann's kisses and touch.

"Baby, I love you," Trese told Vann.

"Um, I love you too boo," he told her while still caressing her body. Trese then slowly turned around and laid on her back. Vann got on top of her and started kissing her slowly and passionately. As he kissed her body, she felt more entwined in the moment. Vann kissed Trese in all the right places and she didn't want him to stop. Her body was saying yes, but her mind was saying shouldn't you have had enough. All he could hear from the sound of her voice was, Oooo, baby you feel so good. Please stop. Constantly moaning from the touch of Vann's tongue, Trese felt as if she and Vann hadn't been together for a while. He released the stress from her physical to her emotional.

After Vann pleasured Trese, they both cuddled and slept through the night. Trese was finally relaxed and she really didn't want to get into her situation with Vann until she had her results back. Having the fall out between her and Tremaine, she still had a lot on her mind.

She finally fell into a deep sleep and started to dream. She dreamt that she was in a room filled with people and they were all whispering to each other. As she looked at everyone, she finally saw some people that she recognized. It was Vann and Darren and they looked straight at her with this confused look on their faces. Suddenly, Trese found herself on the ground begging Vann to forgive her and saying that she was sorry. Trese started crying in her sleep. "Hey, hey, hey baby wake up," Vann said as he pulled on her to wake her.

"I'm sorry baby. What happened?" she asked him while wiping her face.

"Well, it looked like you're crying in your sleep. What's the matter?" he asked her.

"Nothing. I'm fine. Just a bad dream, I guess," Trese hurried up and said. She really didn't want to talk about it.

"Are you okay ma?" he asked her.

"Yes baby, I'm okay," she said as she smiled and then kissed him on the lips. Then Trese got up to go to the bathroom and Vann laid back down assuming everything was okay. Trese went into the bathroom and then locked the door behind her. She glanced in the mirror and asked herself why did I cheat when I knew I had a good man. As the tears rolled down her cheeks, she knew deep down inside that her results would come back positive because she slipped. What have I done, Trese said softly as she kneeled down by the toilet. Trese felt as if she was at her breaking point and she had to release.

After the crying and feeling of guilt, the night passed, and then the weekend passed by really slow. Monday and Tuesday came by really fast and Thanksgiving was just around the corner.

Tuesday was the day for Trese to receive the answers she had been waiting on and the time was ticking like a bomb, ready to explode in Trese's head. She was allowing the time to stress her out because she knew there would be consequences if she heard the unthinkable. Nonetheless, Trese got herself together and headed to the clinic so she could move forward in her life.

After she made it to the clinic, Trese checked in and sat in the lobby for ten minutes before Dr. Velez finally called her

# Circles

to the back. Trese took a deep breath as she desperately tried to read her doctor's facial expression, but she couldn't. Dr. Velez didn't frown or smile. She maintains her straight face. "Have a seat Trese. How are you feeling today?" Dr. Velez asked her.

"I'm okay. Just ready to know what the results are looking like," Trese said.

"Well, let's see. I haven't looked at your file yet," Dr. Velez said as she went through Trese's file. Finally, Dr. Velez looked at the results. "Well Trese, it looks like you have tested positive for HIV. Now this doesn't mean that you're going to get sick or die or anything like that. You're just infected with the virus and it's not curable, which you should already know. However, there are medications which can help you and whomever else you think might possibly be infected," Dr. Velez told her.

As soon as Trese heard her doctor say that she had the virus, all of the other things that were said had faded into a blur of words. Trese held her head down and her heart felt so wounded that she didn't want to hear anymore of what her doctor had to say. "Damn it! Damn it! Dr. Velez, I know that can't be right! How could this have happened to me? I'm supposed to be that person that this just doesn't happen to. This is not supposed to be happening!" Trese screamed in anger as the tears rolled down her face. Dr. Velez gave Trese a hug and told her that everything was going to be okay and that there was help out there for her. Trese still wasn't listening as she was very upset. With what she had just learned about herself, there was nothing that could possibly make her feel any different or better. Being infected with the HIV virus wasn't a dream come true; it was a total nightmare.

Trese couldn't take it anymore. She stopped hugging Dr. Velez and then ran out of the clinic in tears. She got into her car, slammed the door, and started beating the steering wheel.

"Why? Why? Why? Why is this happening to me? I don't know what I'm going to do!" Trese was in total shock. She sat in front of the clinic while her phone constantly rang. Dr. Velez was trying to talk to her because she wanted to make sure she was okay. Then Peaches called her to see what happened at the clinic. Trese was still in shock and she didn't want to talk to anyone. She had only one person on her mind and that was

Vann. Her love, the man she wanted to settle down with
and have a family with. But, all of those dreams were shattered
because of her mistake of sleeping around.

After thinking about what she was going to tell Vann,
she finally drove away heading towards her parents house. On
her way there, Trese's mind was so occupied with deep thought
that she didn't realize it when she ran a red light.

"Newsflash! Newsflash! This is an emergency
broadcast. There has been an accident at the intersection of
Buckner and Samuell Blvd. Traffic will be heavy due to the
emergency vehicles. This has been a news update on 97.9 The
Beat Home of the Rickey Smiley Morning Show." Vann heard
the traffic reporter while he was on his way to his last job. He
tried to call Trese but her phone went straight to voicemail. So,
he just left her a message telling her to call him back. He was
just thinking about her and wanted to know how her day was
going and to tell her how much he missed and loved her.

Trese was out cold inside her car with a head injury
and bruises on her arms and neck. An F150 truck hit her from
the side damaging most of her car. The ambulance hurried and
pulled her out and then rushed her to Doctors Hospital. Her
purse and her phone were slung to the back of her car. By
the time the police searched her car for any of her personal
belongings, she had ten messages.

After she was placed in intensive care at the hospital,
they brought her things and contacted her parents. Trese's
parents had not heard from her since last month. Getting the
bad news about their daughter wasn't the news they wanted to
hear. They rushed to the hospital along with her three brothers.


WHEN HER FAMILY arrived, they talked to the police and the
doctors told her parents that she wasn't responding verbally but
her vital signs and her heart rate was responding perfectly.
Trese's mother broke down into tears. She didn't know how
to accept the fact that her daughter was in intensive care. Her
father was trying to stay strong for the family. Desmond who
was 25, Branden who was 23, and Mico who was 19 were also
doing all that they could do to stay strong for their mother and
their father.

# Circles

Desmond asked his mother to see Trese's phone so she gave it to him. When he turned the phone on he saw all of the missed calls on her phone. "Dang! She has voice messages B," Desmond told Branden.

"Check em and go through her phone and call that girl…what's her name?" Branden asked.

"Yeah, Peaches. Talking about that girl…you know that's her best friend," Mico said while laughing.

"Aight," Desmond said. Desmond then went through her messages. After listening to all her messages, he contacted everyone who left her one. First Desmond called Peaches, then Vann, Tremaine, Dr. Velez, Gena, and then her job. Contacting all Trese's people, Desmond did not know who they really were, but he knew that they had to mean something to his sister.

"Man, everyone that left sis a message sounded real concerned for her," Desmond mentioned to his brothers.

"Why? Did they say anything for you to think that?" Mico asked.

"No, but her doctor was one of the ones who left her a message and now I'm wondering is sis really alright." Desmond started getting a little more concerned wondering if something else was wrong with his big sister.

"Damn it sis! Bro it's gunna be aight. We can't let mom and pops know about this right now. I mean we have to be strong for them," Branden said.

"You're right bro and I'm good…I'm good," Desmond said calmly. As time passed by, the people that Desmond contacted start showing up. First Peaches, Chase, and Gena showed up as soon as they heard the news. Peaches was in tears and when she saw Trese's mother and father she hurried over to them. Peaches had so many questions and she really wanted to make sure her best friend was okay. Trese's mother explained everything to Peaches that the doctor had explained to her. After talking to Trese's mother, Peaches gave her a hug and then went back over to where Chase and Gena were. She explained to them exactly what Trese's mother told her. While Peaches was talking to Chase and Gena about Trese, the doctor came back out with some more shocking news.

Trese's mother broke down to the floor after learning that her daughter had HIV. She couldn't take any more

130

devastating news. Desmond, Branden, and Mico ran to their mother's side and consoled her. Her father was speechless and silently in shock. It was like he couldn't move at all as he stared at his daughter.

Trese opened her eyes noticing that her father was there with her and then she closed them back. He smiled because he knew that his daughter was going to make it out of this one way or another. By the way Trese's mother reacted after the doctor left, Peaches kind of had a feeling that she knew what he told her. Peaches turned around and cried even harder and then told Chase and Gena what else Trese had going on with her as far as the HIV thing.

Vann and Darren finally showed up, walking into all of the commotion. "What happened? What's wrong?" Vann asked.

"Man, shit fool…my nigga let me talk to ya for a minute." Chase hurried and took Vann and Darren to the other side of the waiting area. Chase then explained to Vann and Darren what happened to Trese. Vann broke down. He dropped to his knees. He was so hurt to hear that his girl had been in a car accident and he wasn't there to protect her.

After Chase told Vann about the accident, Peaches and Gena told him the rest. Chase didn't want to see Vann's face when he found out that his girl had HIV. As Vann listened to every word that Peaches and Gena said, he slowly placed his hands over his face and then walked away. Vann couldn't believe what he had just heard. As Vann walked away from everyone, Darren walked right behind him knowing that his homeboy was truly hurting inside and he had to be there for him.

"Man! Fuck! Fuck dawg!" Vann shouted as he hit the wall with his fist. "I can't believe I'm caught up in this shit again! What tha fuck D! What did I do to deserve this shit?!" Vann said as he broke down in tears. Darren couldn't say anything. He really didn't know what to say to Vann. He then gave Vann the tightest hug he had ever given anyone. He wanted his homeboy to know that he was not alone in this. Darren talked to Vann and told him that he still has a life and that he still has him for a best friend no matter what type of shit he was in.

"Man, my nigga you good. This is just news fo' real!"

131

# Circles

Darren tried to be positive about the whole thing, but Vann already knew that his fate was all said and done.

"Nah bro, I'm not good. Shit they say that she has the virus that means I have it too D. Man I need to see her fool! She gotta explain this shit to me my nigga! What tha fuck and who in tha fuck she was messing around with! Damn D! This is some fucked up shit and when I say tha mutha fucking game has been played, my nigga, tha mutha fucking game has been played!" Vann was getting more upset than calm. Vann and Darren walked towards Trese's room and then stared at her through the glass window.

"Why baby? Huh? What did I do Trese? What tha fuck happened?" Vann had all types of questions; hoping that Trese would wake up so he could get some answers. He cried and cried and then he started to wonder what happened and where did he go wrong.

Trese's family never really had a chance to meet Vann. They just heard a lot about him. Trese's mother noticed Vann crying and pouring his heart out to Trese and she knew right then and there that he was Vann. She went over to him and gave him a motherly hug like he was one of her own. Vann didn't know who this woman was, but he really did need a hug and he hugged her back. After she hugged him, she spoke to him and then she and Darren left him to be alone. She walked over to the other side of the waiting area with her husband and sons.

Vann was sobbing and letting his anger out through the window. That's when the elevator dinged and then opened to an unexpected surprise.

"Tremaine...," Peaches whispered.

"Who?" Chase asked her with a confused look on his face. As Tremaine and his cousin walked by, Peaches couldn't hold herself together. She approached Tremaine and grabbed him by the arm before he could go any further.

"Say, lil' mama. Do I know you?" Tremaine asked Peaches while frowning. He then snatched away from her and, just when he was about to take another step, Vann turned his head away from the window and made eye contact with Tremaine for the first time. Vann did not know who he was, but he was curious because of Peaches' reaction when she saw him.

Tremaine looked back at Vann with this devilish grin on his face because he already knew who Vann was. Chase pulled Peaches away from Tremaine.

Trese was still in the same state so her parents were still seated in the waiting area patiently waiting for the doctor to come out with some more information on her. Her brothers were standing near her room watching everything and everyone who arrived. "Fuck! Shit! Fuck!" Desmond said in a low tone. Mico looked at his brother wondering who else he called. Desmond told Mico that he thought he called everyone that left Trese a message.

"Damn nigga!" Mico started laughing because he knew his brother had stirred up some shit, like always.

"What's so funny? This is not a laughing matter Mico!" Branden told him.

"I know… I'm cool. But, Des did tha fool again bro!"

"Man, shut up!" Desmond said as he walked towards Tremaine.

Desmond knew he had to do something and he had to do it fast. So he went over to Tremaine, and his cousin, and introduced himself. Tremaine was relieved because he didn't know anyone there. All he wanted was to see Trese. However, before they knew it, Chase jumped in front of Tremaine and started tripping. Chase couldn't stand the fact that Peaches wouldn't explain to him how she knew of Tremaine. Honestly, she really didn't know him. Peaches just had a feeling that he was Tremaine by the way Trese use to describe him.

Chase was the jealous type and he couldn't stand being lied to. While Tremaine and Chase were arguing, Vann and Darren overheard them and quickly ran over to see what was going on. Things were getting real heated up when all of a sudden, Chase pulled out his pistol and pointed it straight at Treamaine. "What tha fuck nigga?! You must think I'ma frail ass nigga! You think I must don't know what's going on! Peaches! Bring yo mutha fucking ass ova here and tell me who this nigga is," Chase yelled. Peaches quickly came over crying and then explained to Chase that he was the guy that Trese was cheating on Vann with. Chase grinned.

"Damn, you sho'll know a whole lot about me Peaches. And nigga you pulling a pistol out on me cuz you thought I was yo girl's piece of game!" Tremaine laughed and then his cousin raised his shirt flashing his piece to Chase. Vann was shocked to hear that baby girl had another man.

In the midst of all the commotion, the doctors and nurses suddenly rushed to Trese's room. She had stopped breathing. Her parents and brothers were startled and they all ran right behind the nurses.

While they were trying to see what was wrong with Trese, the nurses politely pushed them back so that the doctors could do their job. After her family was told to wait patiently outside her room, three shots were fired. The people in the waiting area and hallways started screaming and running for cover.

Tremaine's cousin pulled his pistol out, after Vann hit Tremaine in the face with his fist. Vann, Tremaine, his cousin, Darren, and Chase got into a deadly scuffle and that's when Chase fired his pistol trying to aim it at Tremaine; but he missed. That's when Tremaine's cousin aimed and fired not caring who he was aimed at. All of the commotion at the hospital had gotten out of hand. The odds were not in anyone's favor, not even in Trese's.

Heather Jornay Perkins

Circles

## 14. SURPRISING RELIEF

THE HOLIDAYS WERE a drag. But knowing that the year
was about to end, Trese had already made her New Year's
Resolution. After the car accident and finding out that she was
HIV positive, her life completely changed; with the first
change being her break up with Vann. Although they had been
together for a year now, to her surprise, she found that the
break up was for the best. Before the break up, Trese and Vann
had plans on moving in together. Trese loved Vann deeply, but
she also had strong feelings for Tremaine, not knowing that
Tremaine would be the one who would put her in the line of
fire. Trese was blinded and careless. She jeopardized herself, her
ex-boyfriend, and their relationship by trying to have her cake
and eat it too. Now Trese realized that some cake should be left
uneaten.

Trese's cell phone started to ring. She glanced at her
caller ID and noticed that it was her mother. "Hi mama," Trese
answered.

"Hey, baby. Just checking up on you. How are you
feeling?" her mother asked.

"Oh, I'm fine mama. Just reading over my New Year's
Resolution. What are you up to?" Trese asked her mother.

"Well, I'm about to leave work and go meet your father
at the office. What do you have planned for bringing in the
New Year?" she asked.

"Well, I don't know yet. Probably church I'm thinking,"
she told her.

"Oh, okay. Well, I'm going to go ahead and head up
here so I will chat with you later, okay," her mother told her.

"Okay. Talk to you later," Trese said. Trese's mother
checked up on her from time to time; especially after all she has
been through.

# Heather Jornay Perkins

After hanging up with her mother and reading over her New Year's Resolution, she got up to run herself a soothing bubble bath. The hot steam from the bath water started to fog up the bathroom mirror. As Trese was about to get inside the bathtub, she dropped her towel and could see, through the part of the mirror which had not fogged yet, some of her scars that were left from the wreck. Flashbacks start playing over and over in her mind. When she would experience these flashbacks, she would blackout momentarily.

Once Trese regained consciousness, she found herself leaning against the bathroom wall experiencing a major headache. Trese reached into her medicine cabinet, very slowly, and pulled out her prescription her doctor prescribed for her. She took one of the pills and then soaked in her hot steamy bubble bath to relax her nerves. Trese usually had blackouts every so often.

It was already going on three o'clock and Trese had just finished soaking. She had almost forgotten that she was meeting Peaches at Target. They had a management meeting that afternoon at four thirty. Trese was actually excited about the meeting and being able to finally go back to work. She had not been anywhere since the accident; except to therapy. Finally recuperating was over and Trese was ready for anything that would keep her mind off of the fact that she was HIV positive.

Peaches was running a little late because of her long talk she had with Chase. They had a few bumps in the road that needed some attention. Chase and Peaches agreed to have some time apart after what happened at the hospital. They still had feelings for one another but Peaches was okay with them having time apart. Sometimes she reflected on what they had together before all of the drama.

Finally leaving the house, Peaches got into her brand new ride. She had been saving her money to buy a new car. She purchased a 2008 Honda Civic, something that she could afford. Peaches couldn't wait to see Trese. She knew Trese had been through so much so she, and a few other co-workers, planned a welcome back party at the job. Peaches and the rest of the Target associates led Trese on thinking that she had a management meeting; and she was really in for a big surprise.

Chase finished his letter to Greedy after his

137

conversation with Peaches. He started writing Greedy every month to let him know about the things that were going on back at home, and with Gena. Even though they had rough times and there was a lot of drama going on, Chase remembered all the good things that Greedy did for him as a brother. He did forgive Greedy and let the things in the past be the past. He figured that someone should still be around for him because his sister surely wasn't and who could blame her. Chase finished his letter, folded it, and then slipped it into an envelope with a postage stamp. After he sealed the envelope, he sat it on top of the kitchen countertop alongside his watch and rolled up money. Chase was about to jump in the shower when he noticed the door was locked. Gena was still in the bathroom. "Gena! Gena!" Chase yelled while beating on the door.

"What boy?!" Gena yelled back. Gena knew he wanted to get in there and she was just messing with him by waiting an extra five minutes before she let him in. She had one coat of lip gloss left to put on her lips.

"You almost out?!" Chase asked.

"Uh huh," Gena said.

"Good! Cause I got a lot of shit on my plate today. And damn you slow. You been in there forever. You must be…," Chase said.

"Now, uh uh don't even go there Chase," Gena said while opening the door. Chase had his bath towel wrapped around his waist, easing through to the bathroom. "What are you smiling for?" he asked his sister.

"Well, because I see you have picked up some of Greedy's old habits. I'm not trying to tell you what to do, but that's not what that is," she told him.

"Man, girl you tripping," he said while placing his cell phone on the sink and brushing her off. Chase closed the bathroom door and started his shower.

Gena straightened up the living room and kitchen before she left for her interview. She had an interview at the Neighborhood Walmart up the street from their house. "Good luck sis!" he yelled from the bathroom.

"Thanks Chase," Gena said as she walked out the door.

As Chase dried off from his showering, his phone rang. He looked and saw that it was Darren calling.

"What's up with ya boy?" Chase answered.

"Yeah, man do me a favor," Darren said.

"Yeah, what's that?" Chase asked.

"Take Sonya some of that what you got. Man, she keeps calling me and shit! I'm at work right now. Can you do that for me bro?" Darren asked him.

"Yeah, I got you. You good," Chase said and then hung up. Darren called Sonya and told her what was up. She was kind of disappointed because she just knew she was going to get her a quickie.

After Chase got ready, he stopped by the post office and dropped his letter off to Greedy before he headed towards Sonya's place. Sonya had the Monday off from work and, while she was waiting on Chase, her best friend Veronica had just stopped by. They were going to the Galleria to hang out and do some shopping. "Girl, we need to buy our outfits today and start getting ready to break in this New Year," Veronica told Sonya.

"Girl, I forgot that was coming up!" Sonya said as she pinned her hair in a ponytail.

"Well, you know Desmond is having his New Year's Bash at the Sheraton downtown," she told her.

"What! Now that's wassup. He always throwing some kind of party. Is he a party promoter for Dallas or something?" Sonya asked.

"Girl, yeah. And you know we are going to see some of everybody there," Veronica said. They both started smiling.

"Yeah coming!" Sonya shouted. She opened the door and it was Chase. He came right on in and, as soon as he walked through the door, he checked out her crib.

"I see ya Sonya, trying to do your thing. It's nice up in here," Chase said.

"Thanks," she said. Chase and Sonya began chatting and then hurried and gave her the corn. After slipping her the corn, he was just about to leave when Veronica came from the back room.

"Oh hey Chase. Before you leave, I want you to meet my best friend Veronica. Chase this is Veronica and Veronica this is Chase," Sonya introduced them.

"Hey," Veronica said from a far distance. Chase couldn't

believe how gorgeous this girl looked.

"Damn…Veronica you look nice, ma," Chase told her while biting the bottom of his lip.

"Thanks," Veronica responded as her face turned red. She was blushing speechless. It was like she didn't have anything else to say; and that was unlike her because she always had something to say.

"Well, Chase thanks for dropping by," Sonya said.

"Yeah, no problem," Chase smiled and then left.

"Girl, why are you standing there like a lottery number waiting to get picked?" Sonya started laughing. It was funny that Veronica was acting brand new when she was always running off at the mouth about what she would do if a good looking man approached her.

Veronica was in a daze. "Wow, I didn't know I could freeze up like that in front of a guy. I mean I didn't even do that to Desmond when I first met him," Veronica told Sonya.

"Uh huh, whatever," Sonya still had the giggles. She couldn't believe her girl had a lost of words in front of Chase, out of all the people in the world; Chase. Even though Chase was very attractive and wasn't a bad guy, Sonya was just shocked that Veronica was acting like that. She guessed a man could make you do the weirdest things.

While Trese was sitting in Target's parking lot at 4:07, Peaches was already there with everyone getting ready for Trese to come inside. Before Trese got out her car she decided to call Vann just to see how he was doing. Even though they were not together, her love for him never left.


VANN WAS AT work at his desk finishing up some paperwork he had to turn in before he left for the day. His cell phone rang and he saw that it was Trese calling him. He wasn't in the mood to talk to her so he ignored her call. Vann missed her a lot but he couldn't get past what she had put him through.

Trese wasn't surprised that he didn't answer and she didn't even bother to leave him a message. Who was she fooling? She had to either let him go or try to get him back. "Lord, please make this situation better than it is now. I love this man and I just want us to be right with one another." Trese said a littler prayer before she prepared to get out of the car and entered Target.

She took a deep breath and then entered the store. As she walked in, a couple of her co-workers noticed her and happily greeted her with hugs and fulfilling conversations. That little attention really made Trese's heart fill with joy and warmth; something she'd really been needing.

While Trese was talking to some of her co-workers, Peaches and all of the management staff were finishing up the decorative settings for Trese's surprise.

"Hi...Trese is it?" Sig asked her.

"Yes, that's me! Are you new?" she asked Sig.

"Yes, ma'am. I am, how'd you know?" he asked.

Trese started to laugh. "Well, because I've never seen you up here."

"Right, gotcha. That was funny. Well, I'm actually your new assistant manager," Sig told her.

"Oh, ok. I didn't know they hired a new assistant manager. And I most definitely didn't know they assigned me to Logistics. That's great! Nice to meet you...," Trese said.

"Oh, I'm sorry, Sigmond Duvay. But, you can just call me Sig," he told her while smiling.

Trese smiled back. "Oh, okay. Well. Let me get upstairs to this meeting. Are you going to the meeting?"

"Yeah," Sig said. Trese and Sig both went upstairs and everyone who was in the break room were waiting patiently for Trese to walk through the door. "Surprise!" everyone shouted. Trese couldn't believe her eyes. She was surprised.

"Wow! All of this for me. You all are so wonderful. I wasn't...," Trese was about to finish her sentence, but Peaches cut her off.

"I know you weren't expecting this, but you deserve it because you are a good manager and we know you've been through a lot."

"Awww..." Trese gave Peaches a hug and a couple of tears rolled down her cheeks. Peaches was the best friend that Trese ever had. No matter what Trese was going through, her girl always came through.

The party was a shocking surprise for Trese. She was overwhelmed with hugs, fulfilling conversations, and gifts.

# Circles

Because of the love and support, she finally felt a bit more relieved from her stress and being at work with her friends made her feel a whole lot better.

Although things were looking a little better for her, Vann was still bitter. After finishing up at work, Vann decided to go straight to the house. He was supposed to go and kick it with Chase and Darren at the pool hall on Lake June. As soon as Vann made it to his apartment, he grabbed him a beer from his refrigerator, turned his television on, sat on the couch, and took his work boots off. He tried to relax but his mind was heavy wondering why Trese called him after all this time. He hadn't heard from her since November.

Vann finished his beer and then dozed off. He was exhausted from work. Vann wasn't trying to fall asleep as he had planned on calling Trese back to see what she wanted. As soon as he dozed off, his phone rang and it was his mother. Vann was trying really hard to avoid talking to anyone, even his family. He didn't even go home, to Kansas where his parents live, for the holidays because he was too ashamed of his situation.

His mother and father left him message after message and still Vann never answered. "Hey baby. This is mama calling you. I've been trying to reach you. Is everything okay with you honey? I only got that one phone call from you saying that you weren't able to make it for the holidays. Please call me and your father. We want to hear from you." Vann listened to his voice message that his mother left him. He couldn't hold it in any longer. He finally broke down and let out all of what he had built up inside.

Everyone was trying to reach him that night, Darren, Chase, and even Chenelle. Chenelle was just checking up on him. She wasn't aware of what happened since she left. Chenelle was in Atlanta on another business trip and this time it was for a lawyers event.

After getting her meds together, eating right, and exercising, she was doing a little better. She started seeing a psychiatrist because she knew it was going to be a while before she would be able to cope with what happened to her. She had a few friends in Atlanta that she made contact with. She wasn't the only one in Atlanta that had escaped the chaos back in Texas. Six was also living his new life like nothing ever happened. Atlanta was his home and bringing old baggage with him just wouldn't mix with his new life, so he thought.

Circles

## 15. SOMETHING NEW

SIX'S ALARM CLOCK was just a buzzing when he finally reached over and hit the snooze button. He laid there for about ten extra minutes with his arm hanging from the bed. Six finally got out the bed, turned the alarm completely off, turned his stereo on, started his coffee, and then ran his shower. This was his daily, Monday through Friday, routine. After he showered, he shaved and then put on one of his casual business attires that he just got out of the cleaners.

Six had a productive career at the airport in the Human Resource Department. Even though his past life was a bunch of bull, he had a degree in Human Resource Management. He was one of the lucky ones that never got caught in the check biz. Before he left Dallas, he was in a whole lot of mess that could one day come back to bite him in the ass. But he handled his situation and moved on.

Six's phone began to ring so he turned his phone display screen on and saw that it was his friend Ani. Ani was a nice, clean-cut brother who worked alongside Six, that he had a fetish for.

While looking into the camera, Ani immediately began to speak. "Hey boo I thought you left already. Well, I'm glad I caught you. I will be running a little late this morning. I have to take care of some important business matters, but I will miss you." Six started laughing because Ani could be so dramatic at times.

"Alright, alright. I'm about to leave in a minute. I had a few things that I needed to get together. But, yeah that's cool. I will see you there," Six said.

"That's cool, but is that all you have to say to me?" Ani asked.

"Ani, man I will see you later aight," Six told him.

## Heather Jornay Perkins

"Um...Okay, whatever." Ani then clicked off the line and Six finished sipping his coffee and then gathered the rest of his paperwork to put inside his briefcase.

When Six got in his car and pulled out of his garage, he saw that his tank was on empty so he stopped at the nearest gas station to fill up. After paying for his gas, Six was walking out of the BP gas station very slowly across the parking area. As he headed towards the gas pump where his car was parked, he reached into his pocket to put his wallet back when his lighter fell out. Before he was able to reach down and pick it up, a young beautiful woman picked it up for him.

"Here you go," she said while handing Six his lighter.

"Oh, thanks ma'," he said, looking directly into her eyes. Six slightly smiled at her and then walked to his car and started pumping his gas.

While at the pump, the young lady came back and started flirting with him on the cool. Six couldn't do anything but enjoy it. He was flattered.

After staring at the young lady, she began to look awfully familiar to Six. So after he gassed up, he went over and asked her name. She told him Che'.

"Che'...hmmm, okay. Well, my name is Six and it was nice to have run into you," Six told her. Before he got into his car to leave, Che' handed him her business card.

Six looked down at her card and read it. "Chenelle Jones...Paralegal, cool," Six said. Chenelle smiled and then went back to her car and they both pulled off. Chenelle was headed to the lawyer's event at the Atlanta Marriott Marquis. There were going to be a lot of paralegals and attorneys there that she wanted to get acquainted with.

*Chenelle... man that name sounds so familiar*, Six said to himself.

He finally made it to work around 9:30 a.m. and, as soon as he got to his desk, he noticed an envelope on his desk that said To: Mr. Cedrick Calhoun From: Ms. Gena Mathis. Six was surprised to even hear from her since what happened. He didn't open the envelope right then because he wanted to wait until later on after he got off of work. He knew Gena must have wanted something because it wasn't like they were best of friends.

# Circles

Despite the letter, Six went ahead and started his day off to a good start. He started it off with conducting an interview and moved on to creating new files for all the employees at the airport. It was a long steady job, but someone had to do it.

After the lawyer's convention, Chenelle and one of her friends, BeBe, met up at this restaurant called Wildfire where they served steaks and seafood. Chenelle and BeBe met on MySpace and this was their second time meeting. BeBe was a lesbian and Chenelle wasn't clueless about that at all. Since it was a man that screwed up her life, she wanted to experience that life with her. BeBe was gorgeous. She was smooth brown complexion with light brown eyes and had water waved hair, which she always kept in a bun. She was dressed in a sassy way with tight jeans and a tight fitted blouse. She topped her outfit off with bad ass designer Gucci stiletto black boots. Girl was killing every chic in there with her wardrobe. Her make-up was lightly set and she had a tongue ring with a couple of tattoos. BeBe was a very attractive young lady and she knew that she could catch any man out there; that's if that's what she really wanted. "Muah. Muah. Hey baby," BeBe said to Chenelle.

"And hugs and kisses to you too." They both greeted each other before they were seated at the bar.

"So, what's been up?" Chenelle asked her.

"Nothing…wow you look nice today. Listen, I was thinking that after we eat, we could go back to my place and talk a bit," BeBe suggested.

"Thanks BeBe. You look nice as always. And okay we can go back to your place. I don't have anything else on my agenda," Chenelle said with a giggle. Chenelle and BeBe had a nice time at Wildfire. They had a few drinks and then left. Chenelle was a little nervous because she had never been with a woman and she couldn't believe that she had actually agreed to doing this.

Before Chenelle got out of the car, she noticed that she had a missed a call from Vann. He didn't leave her a message, so she tried to call him back; but he didn't answer. Chenelle didn't leave him a message either thinking that he would call her right back.

She initially thought that the missed call would have

been from Six, but it wasn't. Six was too busy at work trying to finish up for the day. Ani had already finished for his day and was ready to leave work. He came over to Six's office. "What's up?" Six asked him as Ani stood in the doorway of his office.

Ani stared at Six for a second and then asked him, "Do you want to hook up after work?"

"I don't know. I'm a little beat," Six told him. Ani looked disappointed because this was Six's second time blowing him off.

Six wrapped things up at work. He had Gena's letter sitting on top of his briefcase. Ani looked down and saw the letter. He looked at Six and then asked him what was she doing writing him. Six didn't answer Ani because he liked to keep it professional while he was in the work place. Six just stood up, walked out the office, and headed towards the parking garage while he left Ani standing in the doorway with an upset look on his face. Ani was upset because of the way Six was acting towards him, so he took it the way he wanted to take it; in the wrong way.

On his way home, Six knew that Ani was following him because he knew that Ani was a revenge type of guy; you get at him and then he gets back at you. But Ani didn't know that he was playing with fire because what Ani didn't know was that Six was HIV positive. In the back of Six's mind, he knew that sooner or later the truth was going to come out. He was going to have to confess it to Ani in some kind of way. He knew it wasn't going to be easy dealing with Ani, it never was.

As soon as they both made it in the parking garage and parked, Ani hopped out his car quickly. "Oh yeah Six. That's how we doing things now? I mean damn, you haven't said so much as two words to me at work today and then you gonna walk off on me!" Ani was fired up.

"Damn Ani! We at the job bro. And yeah, I'ma keep it professional at the job. I don't like everyone in my personal business, you know. You should already know how I am. We've been dealing with each other for over two years now. You know what your problem is? You trip too much," Six told him in a low tone while up close on him.

Ani backed away. "Me, tripping? What the fuck eva!"

147

# Circles

There was a few seconds of silence. Ani had his head held down.

Six stared at him and then started walking towards his condo. "Come on man," Six said. Ani followed behind him, still a little heated up, but he wasn't going anywhere because his love for Six was a surprise to him every day.


CHENELLE NEVER RECEIVED that call back from Vann. She thought about him from time to time because that's the man she used to care so much for. Since Vann, Chenelle was not the one trying to love again.

After being inside BeBe's apartment for about 15 minutes, Chenelle was trying to play it cool like she wasn't nervous at all. But, she really didn't know what to expect from BeBe. BeBe came out of her room and asked Chenelle if she want to take a shower first. "I thought we were just going to talk?" CHENELLE asked.

"Anytime a female asks you to come back to their place to talk after you've already talked, it usually means that she wants you to either stay the night or just enjoy your moment with her," Bebe responded. So Chenelle didn't hesitate. She agreed to take her shower first. BeBe gave her some boxers and a tank top and then told Chenelle to make herself comfortable. She could see that Chenelle was a little nervous.

After Chenelle took her shower, BeBe got in and that's when Chenelle took some time to think. She had many thoughts about herself including questioning herself. Her first question was was she really going through with this.

Still in her own little zone, BeBe had already finished her shower and came out of the bathroom. Chenelle was laid across Bebe's bed and, to her, Chenelle was looking like a sweet piece of candy; ready to be eaten. BeBe didn't waste any more time. She turned the lights off and started at Chenelle's feet. She kissed and caressed her feet, legs, and thighs, making Chenelle wonder why did she need a man. After BeBe kissed and caressed her, Chenelle turned on her back and they started kissing each other very passionately. BeBe wanted Chenelle to have a good experience with her, so she treated Chenelle's body as if she really appreciated it, and she did.

# Heather Jornay Perkins

After all the kissing and caressing, BeBe went down on her. The experience for Chenelle was a total shock because she never would have thought that a woman could make her have multiple orgasms. Chenelle moaned and sighed as BeBe worked her magic and wasn't expecting anything in return. That night for BeBe was all about pleasing Chenelle and BeBe was satisfied by doing just that. After all of that, they both fell asleep cuddled in each other's arms, quietly sleeping.

It was midnight and Six and Ani were still up talking. Ani knew it was getting late, but he was where he wanted to be. They didn't go to bed until after one in the morning. Six and Ani knew they had to get up early for work, so they both just called it a night. As the night passed morning shortly came, Six got up before Ani. He did his daily routine, made coffee, took his medicine, and ironed his work clothes. But, he did one thing different that morning; he opened up the mysterious letter from Gena. The letter read:

*Dear Six,*

*I want to start off by saying that there are a lot of things that we still haven't discussed. I have some more questions and I need answers. I know you're wondering how I know of your where about. Well Tank told me. Don't get mad at him for telling me because it was for a good reason. I'm still kind of puzzled about what happened between you and my ex (Greedy). And I really want to know how you're dealing with the fact that you have HIV. I know that I've been taking care of myself, but I'm still taking it hard. I know moving back to your hometown was your best move. You must feel a little relieved from all the drama that happened back here in Dallas. Well, if you don't mind, I would like for you to call me please. (214) 555-2323. Just want to talk.*

*Sincerely, Gena Mathis*

Six was shocked to read a letter like that from Gena; and now she wanted the truth about him and Greedy. He thought to himself how could he explain what happened. He knew she was looking for some kind of confirmation and he knew it would hurt her even if she knew exactly what went

# Circles

down between them. Six had a lot to think about before he even made that call to her.

He folded the letter and placed it back inside the envelope. While, placing the letter inside his junk drawer, he heard Ani getting up. Ani had just came out the bathroom. Six laid back down and he wanted Ani to lay back down with him. Ani knew exactly what Six wanted that morning as they both had a rush of excitement.

Time was still ticking and Chenelle and BeBe were still in bed. Chenelle opened her eyes and couldn't believe that she slept so well. "Um, did you sleep good baby?" BeBe asked.

"Baby?" Chenelle whispered to herself. BeBe started laughing because she knew that Chenelle was new to all of this. Chenelle smiled and then BeBe got up and cooked breakfast for Chenelle before she got her day started. So far so good. Chenelle knew that she would enjoy this a little bit too much.

Heather Jornay Perkins

Circles

## 16. OUT WITH THE OLD, IN WITH THE NEW

IT WAS NEW Year's Eve, a Wednesday, and a day to kick out the old and begin with the new; and Trese was doing just that. Her New Year's Resolution was to move on with her life either with Vann or without him. Her mind was made up to do for herself and to make herself happy, and she was going to start with keeping up with her clinic appointments and make sure she took all of the medication she needed to keep her life going.

Trese was at her apartment still trying to figure out if she was going to celebrate New Year's at church or at her brother Desmond's New Year's Eve bash. She knew that it was a possibility for her to see Vann at the party, so her decision was made. Trese was going to the party.

Trese tried calling Desmond, but he didn't answer. She then tried calling Branden and he didn't answer his phone either. Being that the party was in a few hours, Desmond and a couple of the other party promoters had to make sure everything was ready for the party.

Her final attempt was to contact her baby brother Mico. She finally got an answer, but it was not who she wanted to talk to. "Hello," Tara answered. Tara was Mico's college girlfriend.

"Hi. May I speak to Mico?" Trese asked her.

"To Mico? He is in the shower. Who is this?" Tara asked.

"Well, if you looked at the caller ID then you would have noticed that I'm Mico's big sister, Trese," Trese told her in a fly manner. Trese hung up in Tara's face. She couldn't believe Mico had some broad answering his phone.

"Yo. Who was that on the phone T?" Mico asked while drying his head off.

"I didn't know who it was at first. It turned out to be

Trese, your sister," Tara told him while frowning.

"Ole sis. I knew she would call around this time," Mico said. Tara looked at Mico confused because she never knew he had a sister. He never told her that he had one, and that made her feel unimportant.

Mico sat on the bed after slipping on his boxer briefs and then he called Trese back.

"Sis!" Mico said with a happy tone in his voice.

"Hey baby brother! Now question. Who was that girl who answered your phone while you were in the shower?" Trese asked him.

"Oh. That's my girl Tara. Yeah my bad sis. She didn't know about ya," Mico explained.

"Um. You must not be serious with this one?" Trese asked while laughing.

"Maybe maybe, still have some more things to check out, then we'll see," he said.

"Oh, okay. Whatever you say. I was trying to catch up with Des and Branden but they're not answering their phones," Trese told him.

"Oh yeah. Des is at the Sheraton doing some last minute stuff and Branden is at the barbershop. I don't know why he didn't pick up. Ohhh…he must be in the chair. So you must be coming to the party?" Mico asked her.

"Yes I am. Matter of fact, let me make sure Peaches is going," she said.

"Aight big sis. Just hit me back. Shit I'm bout to head up to the cleaners and to the barbershop myself," Mico told her.

"Okay I will. Bye boy!" Trese said and then hung up and called Peaches.

Peaches was going to the party, but had not checked with Trese yet because she didn't think Trese would be up to it. So when Trese called Peaches to make their plans for the evening, Peaches was just leaving the nail shop. After they finalized their plans, Peaches went back to her place to catch a nap before the party and Trese went shopping for an outfit because she had to look fly if Vann was going to be there.

On the way to the barbershop, Mico ran into Vann and Darren at the 1Stop Shop right next door to Knockouts. "What up V and Darren?" Mico slapped hands with them and then

# Circles

asked if they were coming to the party.

"Yeah, we going little bro. About to get g'd up now, you know," Vann said. After Vann and Darren finished talking to Mico, they both left headed towards Big T Bazaar and Mico went on inside Knockouts to get his haircut. Tara had dropped him off and she headed to the beauty shop to get her hair done.

Mico and Tara had been together since the beginning of the semester of their Freshman year at the University of North Texas. She was majoring in Fashion Design and Mico was still undecided. The only thing that Mico was for certain about was being with Tara; however Mico was not privy to the fact that his girl's source of income came from her night job as a stripper.

After Mico finished getting his haircut, he and his brother Branden left and went back to the house to finish getting ready for the party. Tara was almost done at the hair salon when she got a call from Tremaine. "Hey babe," she answered.

"What's up with ya? Where you at?" Tremaine asked her.

"Oh, just about to leave the salon. What's up?" she asked.

"Come and slide through here right quick. I need to holla at ya for a min," Tremaine told her.

"Okay. Are you back at the spot?" she asked him.

"Yeah. Just come on through," he said.

"Alright, I'm on my way," she said while paying the hairstylist for her services. When Tara was on her way to the spot where Tremaine was, she noticed that she had a hickey on her neck from Mico. "Damn!" she mumbled under her breath.

Tremaine was in the spot in South Dallas on Stoneman where he always hung out at. Tara pulled up in front of the house and blew her horn for him to come out. Tremaine came out and got in the car with Tara. When he leaned over to give her a hug he noticed the hickey on her neck. "What tha fuck is that?!" Tremaine shouted while grabbing her by the neck.

"Boy, stop grabbing me like that! See that's why I haven't been around you because you are too aggressive," she told him.

"Shit! I don't give a fuck. Who put that shit on your

154

neck? You been fucking off on me just like that T!" he said. Tremaine couldn't even talk to Tara anymore because he had to catch himself too many times before hitting her, so he got out the car and slammed the car door. As soon as he slammed the door, Tara burned off without saying goodbye to him.

It was getting late in the evening and everyone was still trying to get situated for the party. Desmond finally made it back to the house and gave his brothers their hotel room keys so they could crash at the hotel after the party was over. "Say Des. Sis was looking for you earlier," Mico told him.

"Oh yeah, what did she want?" Desmond asked.

"I guess about the party. She said she was going," Mico told him.

"Aight, I'll call her in a min," he said. Desmond took a quick shower and got himself together a little early because he had to be there before the guest arrived.

Mico called Tara to see if she got the things she needed for herself for the party. As he was calling her, she was already pulling up. Tara had to straighten herself up before she came into the house. She didn't want Mico to think that something was wrong.

When Tara came in, Mico was sitting on the couch playing his PS3 game. As soon as he saw her walk through the door, he got up and went to hug her and kiss her. "Baby your hair looks nice. Yeah girl. You did that boo," he told her.

"Thanks baby." Tara tried to keep a smile on her face.

After Desmond finished getting ready, he called Trese. "Hey girl!" he said while throwing some cologne on his neck.

"Hey D. Did Mico tell you that I was trying to get in touch with you?" she asked.

"Yeah, he told me. So I should see you at the party tonight, huh?" he asked.

"Yes. Me and Peaches are coming. And don't worry, your sister will be looking right," she said while laughing.

Desmond started laughing. "Girl you crazy. But, yeah I'm about to head up there now. You know a lot of us have to be up there before the guests arrive. O' yeah, I have your hotel key too; that's if you were planning on staying at the hotel after the party," Desmond told her.

"Hell yeah I am! Thanks baby. You know how to treat

your sister right," Trese said.

"Aight then sis. Let me get out of here and I will see you later," he said.

"Okay, that's wassup," she said as she hung up.

After Desmond hung up with Trese, he left the house and then stopped by Veronica's place. He rang the doorbell and Veronica came to the door in her slip dress. "What are you doing here?" Those were the first words that came to Veronica's when she saw Desmond at the door.

"What? I'm here to see you. Are you going to invite me in?" Desmond asked her. Veronica let him in and then they both sat down at her kitchen table.

"You act like you're not surprised to see me," he said.

"Oh, and I'm not Des. You have been on my shit list lately and you know that!" Veronica told him.

"Your shit list? Look here baby girl, I was just stopping by to see how you've been. Since we've been spending so much time apart from each other, you've been tripping," Desmond said.

"Me, tripping? No I don't think so Des. Who wanted for us to have some time apart? Yeah! That choice wasn't mine!" she screamed. After all of the back and forth bickering at each other, Desmond finally asked her if they could start fresh and Veronica agreed. That's all she wanted was to be back together.


WHEN DESMOND FINISHED talking to Veronica, he left and she called Sonya and told her what happened. Sonya knew that it was going to happen sooner or later because Veronica and Desmond were too cute together and Desmond knew he had a good woman and Veronica knew she had a good man. Being a well known party promoter, and being in the limelight all the time made her jealous; especially when the females gave him the wrong attention in her face. That was just something Veronica had to deal with if she wanted to be with Desmond.

Sonya tried to reach Darren after hanging up with Veronica, but she didn't get an answer. Darren had left his phone in the car while he and Vann were in Big T. Vann's chain was ready for him to pick up. He purchased a 22kt gold chain with seven diamonds in it. That cost him an arm and a leg, but it was worth it to him.

Before walking out of Big T, Vann bumped into this chic named Larenda. "Excuse you!" Larenda said with an attitude. Larenda was feisty and very outspoken.

"Pardon me," Vann said trying to be funny. Larenda looked at him up and down and noticed that Vann was very attractive.

She started smiling and then asked him, "Is that how you always approach women you don't know?"

"Well, lil mama. I wasn't trying to approach you. I bumped you by accident. What's your name though, ma?" he asked her.

"Uh huh, my name is Larenda. And yours?" she asked him.

"Vann and this is my boy D." After introducing themselves to one another, Larenda decided to give Vann her number and Vann did the same.

"Man. I think ole girl bumped into you on purpose dawg," Darren told Vann.

"You think so? I don't know if she did or not. But she was looking right D," Vann said.

"Yeah lil mama was looking good. But that don't mean you about to get at her. You still hung up on Trese," Darren told him.

Vann started laughing and said, "Man you tripping." Darren and Vann left the Cliff and headed back to Mesquite to Darren's place where Vann left his ride.

Darren noticed that Sonya had been calling him so he called her back. "Hey baby mama," Darren said.

"Boy where you been? I've been trying to reach you!" Sonya said.

"Man, you know I left my phone in the car. I was up at Big T with Vann and I forgot my shit," he told her.

"Um, okay. Anyway, I was trying to see if you were going to be at Desmond's party tonight and if Vann coming?" she asked.

"Yeah, we gone slide through there. I don't even have to ask you. I know you going!" he told her.

"Surely is! Me and Veronica will be up in there doing our thang! Say have you talked to Chase? I need another one,"

# Circles

Sonya said.

"Nah. I haven't, but I got you. Let me hit him up now," he said.

"Okay call me back," she said.

"Aight." Darren called Chase after Vann left to go back to his place to get ready.

"Yo!" Chase answered his phone while sitting on the living room floor watching television.

"Damn bro you been MIA for these past couple of days. Sonya needs another one of those and nigga I know you going to be at the party!" Darren said.

"Yep. I'll be there. But I think Gena has some other plans. I'll slide through Sonya's. Just let her know I'm coming, aight," Chase said.

"Aight." Darren hung up with Chase and called Sonya back to let her know that Chase was coming.

"Hey Gena!" Chase yelled. Gena was in the back, in her room, getting her things together. She was not planning on going to the party. She had something else up her sleeve.

"Yeah!" she yelled back.

"Say, are you going to the party? You know Desmond New Year's Party!" he yelled asking her.

"No I'm not!" she told him.

"Aight then. Well I'm about to head over to Peaches." Chase grabbed his keys and then left. As Gena was sitting on her bed contemplating on her next move, her phone rang and it was Six.

Heather Jornay Perkins

Circles

## 17. THE SET UP

"SIX! I'M GLAD you called," Gena said.

"Right. Well, I read your letter and I will tell you anything you want to know. Just one thing," he said.

"Yeah, what's that?" Gena asked him.

"Do you think you can make it up here by tomorrow if I pay for your air flight? It would be best if we spoke in person than over the phone," he told her.

Gena was shocked to even receive an invitation like that from Six. "Well, yeah, yeah. I will start getting ready now."

"Okay. Well I will set everything up and you will have to just show up and make sure you call me as soon as you make it so I can pick you up," Six told her.

"Okay will do," Gena said. She was actually excited to get away from Dallas herself. She really needed a vacation. Not that it was a vacation; but she needed the time away.

After Six hung up the phone, he finished cleaning up his condo. Ani was out of town with family so Six was cool with Gena coming.

When Six put away the last dish from his dishwasher, his cell phone rang. When he looked at the caller ID, he didn't recognize the number but answered it anyway. "Hello," he said with skepticism in his voice.

"Hey is this Six?" Chenelle asked. She was at her hotel room taking a break from her work and decided to call Six.

"What's going on girl?" he asked her.

"Nothing much. Just taking a break from this paperwork. I was just calling you to see if you were doing anything for the night?" she asked.

"Tonight….oh tonight is New Year's Eve! Man my mind is gone. I've been cleaning up and I completely forgot about that. And no, I'm not. I'm just going to call it a night," Six

160

told her.

"Oh, okay you sound like me," she said.

"You know, it seems like I've seen you or heard of you before. Like your name; I've heard it from somewhere before. I just can't recall," he said.

"Really? Well, I'm originally from Dallas, but now I'm living in Houston going to school there," Chenelle told him.

"Well, maybe that's where I know you from because I just moved up here from Dallas," Six said.

"Oh okay. Well one of my old best friends is named Jewell and we have been friends since grade school," she told him.

"Jewell! Light skinned Jewell?" Six asked.

"Yeah, that's my girl," she said.

"Man this is a small world. I know her. We use to do the check business together. If you know what that means," he said.

"Yeah, I know what that means silly. My old guy friend use to do that with some people. As a matter of fact, his name is Greedy. I know you must know him because he's Jewell's friend too!" Chenelle was getting excited jumping up from her bed but Six got quiet because it all made since to him now. Chenelle was the girl that came back and stirred up all of the mess that had been going on.

"Six? Six? Are you there?" she asked while sitting back down on the bed.

"Yeah, my bad. I'm here. Yeah Greedy. Say Chenelle it would be great if we could meet up for lunch or something tomorrow," he suggested.

"Cool, that sounds like a plan," she said.

"Okay well I will let you know when and where tomorrow morning, if that's okay?" Six asked her. He wanted to make sure he wasn't sounding too different with her.

"That's cool," Chenelle said. So they both hung up and Chenelle went back to doing her paperwork and Six knew he was going to have a dilemma. He couldn't believe it and now his thinking cap was on. He wanted Gena to finally meet Chenelle and that's when he decided that he would tell them what happened with him and Greedy. Six was a dirty worker, but he had to let them know some kind of way. He was tired of hiding the truth and going in circles with everyone. There were some things that just weren't meant to remain quiet.

Chenelle couldn't believe that she and Six knew the same group of people. She started to wonder if Six knew her secret.

Back in Dallas, Gena was at the airport waiting for lift off. She was already seated on the plane and on her way to ATL and did not have a clue about what she was getting herself into. All she knew was that she wanted to get away and that's exactly what she was doing.

WHEN CHASE MADE it to Peaches', they both acted as though they had never split up. They were both getting ready for Desmond's party and playing around with each other. "Man I've missed you so much Chase," Peaches told him.

Chase started smiling and replied, "You know, I miss you Peaches. But I have to build that trust up with you again for us to really work this out."

"I know Chase. I just want you to know that I still care," she said. Peaches then stopped playing with Chase after she saw how serious he was about their situation.

After they finished getting ready, Peaches left before Chase did and met up with Trese at her apartment. Chase grabbed a couple of things and then made his way over to Sonya's.

Sonya was all ready to go, but she was still waiting on Veronica and Chase. Chase made it there before Veronica did. Sonya opened the door. "Damn! Sonya you looking good ma fo' real!" Chase said as he came in and shut the door behind him.

"Thanks Chase. Now where is my green?" she asked him.

"Right here lady." Chase gave her the corn and she gave him his money. Chase smiled at Sonya showing his grill. "You sure Darren knows what you looking like tonight, because if he doesn't, then he is in a world of trouble behind yo ass!"

"Boy shut up and get out of here!" Sonya said while holding the door open. Soon as Chase left, Veronica pulled up. Sonya told her that she had just missed Chase just by minutes. Veronica was looking jazzy herself.

"Ready to bring in the New Year girl? Cause I know I am. I am so happy right now," Veronica said.

"Girl, I know you are now that you and Des have made up. You should be happy," Sonya told her.

"Awww." Veronica and Sonya gave each other girlfriend hugs and then Veronica drove off heading towards the Sheraton.

It was 10:28 p.m. and it seemed as though everyone was making it there at the same time. Trese even invited Sig to come and celebrate the New Year's with her and Peaches.

Everyone knew about the New Year's Eve Bash except Tremaine. He heard about it at the last minute through one of his partners. So, at the last minute, Tremaine decided that he would step out and show his face a little; hoping that he would see Tara there. He wasn't expecting to see anyone else there that he knew.

Tremaine had Sharon on his side. She was just a little dip he would fuck around with every now and then. Sharon was Larenda's friend and she was hoping not to see Tremaine, because she wanted to see some new men that she could talk to. The night was just beginning and everyone was there looking to have a good time. Everyone accept for Tara. She was praying that she would not see Tremaine there at all because she knew how he'd react, seeing her with someone else. And she definitely didn't want to put Mico in the mix like that. Tara was playing with fire and just waiting to get herself burned.

Circles

## 18. DESMOND'S NEW YEAR'S BASH

THE SHERATON'S BALLROOM was set up real nice. The
colors were mixed with gold, silver, and white. The bars were
set up to serve at each corner of the room and the entrée tables
were set up in the middle of the room like a buffet. The DJ was
keeping the music flowing while the dance floor was filled with
people all across the room. "Wow, this place is really nice," Tara
said as she, Mico, and Branden walked in the entrance way of
the hotel.

"You know we got the key to the room after the party
T," Mico told Tara. Tara was all up on her man and not letting
him out of her sight. Branden left the two of them alone since
they were acting like they hadn't seen each other in years.

As people entered into the hotel, party favors were
handed out. "Girl, Desmond and LD are doing the fool! They
are actually giving away Victoria Secret fragrances," Sonya said
to Veronica while holding the bag up in the air.

"Girl, Sonya stop that!" Veronica said as she took
Sonya's arm and pulled her inside the ballroom. After Veronica
and Sonya made it, Trese and Peaches made their way through
the front entrance. Chase was right behind them getting his car
parked by the valet. The entrance way was packed and almost
blocked because all of the people who had shown up at the
same time. It was a showcase of a live fashion show from all of
the models, to the doe boys, to the people with just a little and
the people with a lot. Some of the Dallas Cowboys and the
Dallas Mavericks even showed up.

"D, we put this shit together like nobody else could up
in Dallas…fo' real!" LD told Desmond.

"Fo' real, I feel ya! That's the way it's supposed to be and
that nigga Tweety talking about his shit was the spot tonight,"
Desmond told LD.

164

"Tweety?" LD had no idea who Desmond was talking about.

"You know that nigga up at Club Flow. Man, see nigga you didn't even know who I was talking about and this nigga say he known," Desmond said as he busted out into laughter.

"Oh, ole boy! Man, come on now D. We on a whole notha level than that dude," LD told Desmond.

"Hey, there goes my girl and I must say she looking more gorgeous than ever," Desmond said as he walked away to greet Veronica. Veronica saw Desmond coming towards her and then suddenly turned and saw Chase entering into the ballroom. When she glanced at the entrance, Chase noticed her as well and they stared at each other for a moment. Paying him no attention, Veronica received a kiss on the cheek by Desmond. "What's up?" he asked her while whispering in her ear from behind. Veronica turned around and gave Desmond a hug. "You looking good ma. I just had to come and tell you before these other niggas did." Desmond knew his girl looked good and knew that the other guys would try to holler at her if they could.

Veronica started blushing and said, "Thanks baby." While Veronica and Desmond were talking, Sonya made her way to the bar to get her a drink. Larenda and Sharon arrived right after Chase and then Vann and Darren shortly thereafter.

Trese was looking around trying to see if Vann was there. "Are you looking for someone miss lady?" Sig asked her as he walked up.

Trese and Peaches gave him a hug. "Hey Sig! I was thinking that you weren't going to make it," Peaches told him.

"Nah. I wouldn't miss this party. Looks like this is where it's at!" Sig said while looking at the women passing by. "Excuse me ladies. I need to go and get myself a drink and see who I know; or can get to know," Sig said as he eased his way to the bar.

"OOOO!" Trese accidentally shouted. She spotted Vann and Darren across the room. "Girl, what's wrong with you?" Peaches asked.

"Girl! There goes Vann. I thought I wasn't going to see him tonight," Trese said.

"Girl, stop playing. That was the only reason you came;

trying to see if Vann was going to be here. And what do you know he is here!" Peaches said.

Vann and Darren were across the room enjoying their drinks and all of the women in the room. Larenda knew that Vann was there because she was sitting at one of the tables by the door with her girl Sharon when she saw him walk by. After Vann got his second drink, Larenda decided to go over to him and make conversation. Before he turned around to leave the bar, Larenda tapped him on his shoulder. "Hey you," she said. Vann turned around and was shocked to see Larenda again for the second time. She was stunning.

"Hey. I didn't expect to see you here girl. You looking good. Nah, let me take that back. You looking stunning ma," Vann complimented her. She had on a red sequence fitted dress with a diamond cut. Her diamond trimmed necklace dropped right in the V cut of her dress. She wore silver stilettos and her hair was spiraled curled all over. Her make-up was very nice and her earrings were dazzling. Larenda was rocking it that night.

"Who is that?!" Peaches asked Trese.

Trese took another sip from her glass of apple martini. "Who?"

"That girl over there with Vann," she told Trese.

"I don't know," Trese said.

"Girl you sounding like you don't care. Now wasn't it your idea to come here so you could get your man back! I know you just didn't want to see him." Peaches was acting like she wanted to go over and interrupt their conversation herself.

While Vann was talking to Larenda, Darren and Sonya hit the dance floor and Larenda's friend Sharon was still sitting at the table all by herself. Chase saw Peaches and Trese sitting at the table by the bar, so he walked over and asked Peaches to dance with him.

While the song was playing, it brought back memories for Trese. She didn't want to waste anymore time. She decided to interrupt Vann's conversation he was still having with Larenda. It looked like they were getting too acquainted with one another.

As Trese walked over to Vann and Larenda, they were just about to kiss. She didn't know what to think. It appeared as if Vann was actually trying to move on with his life. So, after Trese got close enough to see, she paused. Vann was so wrapped up into Larenda that he didn't even notice Trese walking over towards him. Larenda and Vann locked lips. This was exactly what he wanted; to meet and mingle with new women. Trese turned around and walked back to her table.

It was like the night couldn't have gotten any worse. As soon as Trese sat back down at her table, Tremaine made a grand entrance with Trese being the first to notice him. Tremaine had his black Gucci shades on, his black Ed Hardy jeans, a white and silver Ed Hardy t-shirt, and some all white Air Forces. He was dripped down and blinging to the T. He pulled his shades down just a little bit to check out the crowd in the ballroom. Trese then put her head down and hurried and texted Peaches to let her know that Tremaine was in the building. Tremaine made his way to one of the bars to get a Hennessey on the rocks. Just so happen that the bar he went to was the one where Trese was sitting.

After Peaches read Trese's text message, she knew Chase couldn't see Tremaine under any circumstance; especially after what happened at the hospital. When Tremaine got his drink, he looked over at the table Trese was sitting and stared as if he'd seen a ghost. Trese didn't want to make eye contact with him so she just got up and walked away from the table. Tremaine grinned and then started to walk around. He knew he and Trese were not cool anymore and he was actually glad that she didn't say anything to him. Peaches pulled Chase to the other side of the room just so he could avoid seeing Tremaine whom she spotted when he was at the bar by Trese.

Trese finally ran into Vann alone. Larenda had already gone back to her table, with Sharon, to give her the juicy details about what happened between her and Vann. Vann spoke first by asking Trese how long she had been at the party because it was almost countdown. "I've been here for a while. I saw you earlier. I just didn't want to interrupt you and your friend girl," she told him.

"My friend girl…oh Larenda. Yeah, I just met her. She aight. So how you been though? I saw that you called me. I wasn't feeling too good when you called. But I'm good now," Vann told her.

# Circles

"Oh, I've been okay. Just taking it one day at a time. And getting myself back to normal," Trese told him as she took a deep breath.

"Yeah, I feel you on that baby girl. You still looking good. I mean, you are looking beautiful tonight," Vann complimented her.

"Wooh!" Sonya said while holding her back and running out of breath. Darren had Sonya on a workout. They had been on the dance floor all night. Trese and Vann were at the table sitting and talking when Darren and Sonya walked up and stood next to the table. Next, Desmond and Veronica came and sat down, joining them. Everyone started to crowd around as it was getting close to count down. Mico, Tara, and Branden came over, and then came LD, Sharon and Larenda, then Peaches and Chase.

Everyone was talking amongst their circles when Tremaine walked by and noticed Tara. When Tara saw him, she had the most frightened look on her face. After Tremaine noticed her, he didn't realize that Sharon, Chase, Vann, Darren, Peaches, Trese, Mico, Branden, and Desmond had laid their eyes on him by this time as well. "Tara!" Tremaine called her name so loudly that Mico heard him. He looked over at Tara and then asked her how did she know Tremaine. Tara was speechless; she didn't know what to say to Mico.

"Tara!" Sharon said. Tremaine looked over at Sharon and then he was like damn.

"Oh hey Sharon," he said. Sharon didn't appreciate how Tremaine was disregarding her presence.

Mico, becoming heated, pulled Tara to the side and then that's when things began to flare up.

"Why in tha fuck is this nigga here?" Chase asked. He was more than ready to beef with Tremaine.

"What nigga?! It's you again! What? You following me now nigga?!" Tremaine asked; ready and willing to do whatever. Desmond and LD hurried and got into the middle of them before there was a bunch of chaos. Desmond and LD escorted Tremaine out of the ballroom and then the police took him away from the hotel. He wasn't allowed back into the hotel... not anywhere close.

"Damn! I can't believe you T! Please tell me that you

didn't sleep with this dude, please…," Mico asked her.

Tara then broke down in tears. "No I have not Mico. I just know him from the strip club."

"The what?! The what, Tara?! You fucking strip?! You never told me you was a stripper!" he screamed at her.

"I know. I know baby. I was going to tell you but I didn't want you to think differently of me." Mico looked at Tara with a blank stare and then turned around and walked away leaving Tara with her own sorrow to drown in.

Trese saw what happened and she knew her little brother was hurt. She told Branden to go after him to see what was really going on while she went over to talk to Tara. "Well, that's why I never got a chance to meet you. My brother is very, very picky about who he brings around his family," Trese told Tara, then walked away. Trese knew that what she said was mean, but it was the truth and Tara needed to hear it if she wanted to get her man back. All Mico ever wanted from Tara was trust; and if they didn't have that, then they had nothing.

"10, 9, 8, 7, 6, 5, 4, 3, 2, 1 Happy New Year!" everyone in the ballroom shouted while wishing one another a Happy New Year. Everyone except for Mico and Tara, that is. Mico decided to spend the rest of the night with his family and Tara left after the countdown.

Tremaine called Tara from the minute he was thrown out of the party but Tara wasn't feeling Tremaine so she declined all of his calls and just went over to her parent's. She couldn't believe the night she had. It was such a mess; a mess that she had to get herself out of and fast. Tara had strong feelings for Mico and she didn't want to lose him. Although Mico was trying to act as though the incident between he and Tara didn't bother him but, deep down, it really killed him.

THE PARTY AT the Sheraton was over at 2:00 a.m. Everyone who was close to Desmond had a hotel key and there were after parties all throughout the different hotel rooms. Mico went back to his room by himself because he had a lot to think about and really wanted to clear his head.

Desmond and Veronica ended up together, but Desmond and LD had a lot of business to finish up before they called it a night. Veronica was right on her man's arm the whole time.

"Girl, I cannot believe Tremaine showed his ass up at this damn party tonight acting a fool as usual," Larenda said to Sharon.

"I know…umm." Sharon had a headache and she really didn't want to talk about Tremaine. Larenda didn't want to say much more herself. She sensed that Sharon was bothered by Tremaine acting like he didn't even know her after all she had been through with him in the past. Larenda dropped Sharon off at her place and, as soon as she pulled off, Tremaine walked up.

"Hey," he said.

"What?" she asked him.

"Look, I just came over to apologize for acting the way I did," Tremaine said.

"Okay." Sharon was not trying to hear Tremaine at all. She opened her door and then she turned around to see if Tremaine was there; he was gone. Tremaine had walked back to his car and headed home.

After Larenda dropped Sharon off, she tried calling Vann, but for some strange reason his line was busy. Vann was still at the hotel with Darren. Peaches and Chase had already left and Trese had gone up to her room where she couldn't even stop thinking about Vann. Darren decided to take Sonya back to her place because Veronica was staying with Desmond for the night, so they left shortly after Peaches and Chase. Vann couldn't stop thinking about Trese either, but he knew that their connection was over and he had to move on.

"Vann what you still doing up here man?" Desmond asked him.

"Yeah, I'm about to leave. Just trying to shake these drinks off," he told Des.

"Well, you know Trese got a room. Ask her if you can crash till morning," Desmond suggested to him.

Vann cleared his throat. "Yeah, good idea bro." Vann called Trese and asked if he could crash in her room since he had too many drinks. Trese was more than happy to let Vann come up to her room.

When Vann knocked on the door, Trese opened it to see the love of her life. "Okay you are loaded," she said while grabbing him to come into her room. As soon as Vann came in, he fell onto the bed and started snoring. Trese laughed and then took his shoes off. After Trese got Vann under the covers, she laid down on the other side of the bed and turned the lamp light off. "Good night Vann," Trese said before she closed her eyes.

The next day, Tara decided to settle for plan B because, the way things were going between her and Mico, plan A wasn't going to be the answer. She had tried calling Mico several times and he still didn't answer any of her calls. Mico was actually at home chilling and playing his PS3. Every time Tara called, he would decline her calls. Mico wasn't trying to hear anything Tara was trying to say because she didn't tell him the truth about her being a stripper. And then, she knew Tremaine out of all people.

"Bro, you ain't gunna at least talk to the girl?!" Branden said.

"Nope! She lied to me bro and most of all that nigga Tremaine, come on now! That nigga stay up in the strip club fucking around and shit. And ain't no telling what tha fuck they have already done. My nigga, she was in violation and just need some time to think." Mico was hot. He saw what his sister went through and be damned if he was going to get caught up in the same situation.

"I feel you on that bro. But say, it won't hurt to see what the case really is. I'm just saying, you two have been together since the beginning of the semester and she cuts for you strong Mico," Branden told him.

"Yeah, I know she does. Man I will call her when we finish this game," he said. Mico knew Branden was speaking on some realness and, deep down inside, he did miss Tara. That was his ace, but he thought their relationship was a lot stronger than what it was.

After Tara called the last time, she finally left a message. "Hey Mico. I know that I lied to you and please forgive me. I never meant for anything like this to happen to us, but it did. You're my man and Tremaine is nothing to me, but a friend. I don't know too much about him. All I know is that I love you and from the day that we met, it's always been you, Mico." Tara poured her heart out to Mico through a voice message.

# Circles

Mico called her after he listened to her asking him for forgiveness. Tara was lying down in her bed, thinking if she should just go over to Mico's to get him to talk, when her phone rang. Surprisingly, it was the person she had been waiting to call her, Mico.

"Mico...Baby," she said answering her phone.

"Yeah. I got your message. Before you get started, just let me say something and hear me out on this T. You know, I thought our relationship was better than what it was portrayed to be; at least that's what I thought. You are my world T and I just don't know if that feeling will ever be the same because you lied to me and if we stay together then I would have to build that trust back up with you and I'm not for sure how long that is going to take. I love you, but it feels like you betrayed me by hiding things," Mico told her.

"Mico, I never meant for this to happen. I met Tremaine at the strip club before I started talking to you and that's all that it is really. I'm sorry for not telling you that I was a stripper. I just didn't want you to think of me as some type of hoe or something. I'm just trying to make more money for college that is it," she said.

"I understand. It's just that when Tremaine called your name, that was a wrap for me because he has HIV and he gave that shit to my sister and that's why all of that shit went down at the party last night. That shit is serious to me and I don't want that to happen to us. That's why when I say I need trust, that's what I mean T," Mico said.

"I understand baby. Please forgive me and I will never, ever speak to Tremaine again and he is deleted from my phone and my memory. I'm not trying to jeopardize anything that we have. You're my boo," Tara told him.

"I am?" he asked her.

"Yes you are," she said. Tara and Mico made up and as soon as they got off the phone Tara left and went straight over to see Mico. She couldn't wait to see him.

Mico's decision was made and it was to go ahead and give it another try because he and Tara really had a special connection between them. It was the beginning of something new for the both of them.

"Ahhh, nigga you made up with her anyway. You

weak!" Branden told Mico while laughing. Mico smiled. "Nah I'm not weak. I just love her too much. But if this shit happens again, then it's over fo' real bro."

"Nigga shut up!" Branden said while walking out the front door.

"Say, where you going bro?" Mico asked him.

"Over to LD's crib," he told him. As soon as Branden drove off, Tara pulled up.

Mico went to the bathroom and Tara was at the door knocking. Tremaine called her while Mico was in the bathroom. "Coming!" he shouted. Tara hurried and declined Tremaine's call just right before Mico came out and let her in.

"Hey baby," Mico said while giving her a hug. Tara grabbed Mico's face and then kissed him on his lips. They kissed for a long time like they were teenagers still in high school making out for the first time. After they kissed, Tara and Mico went to his room and did more than making out since they didn't do the countdown together. They had a New Year's after party of their own.

Circles

## 19. FINALLY THE TRUTH COMES OUT

STANDING IN THE middle of the airport in Atlanta, Georgia, Gena couldn't believe that she had finally made it; new things, a new place, and new people, what else new was there. It was as though she had been waiting on this moment forever. She reached down inside her purse looking for her cell phone, while standing by the baggage claim area. It was 7:00 in the morning and Gena was ready to explore this unfamiliar place.

Gena hurried and called Six. She started to feel a little frustrated because his cell phone just kept on ringing and ringing. On her fifth call, as she waited for the last ring, Six finally picked up. "Yeah?" He answered.

"Hey! I made it!" Gena excitedly told him. Six started laughing because of the enthusiasm in Gena's voice.

"Oh, ok. Give me a minute and I will come and pick you up shortly. Hang tight," he told her.

"Cool," Gena said. After hanging up with Gena, Six got up and washed out his morning breath, washed his face, and then slipped on a pair of wrinkled jeans and a plain white tee-shirt. It was New Year's Day and this was the day Six was suppose to be resting but he didn't mind because today was important to him. This was the day to finally tell the truth about what happened with him and Greedy.

While Gena was waiting on Six, she went by Starbucks to get a Café Chocolate Latte. After she got her coffee, she then walked over to the baggage claim area and Googled on her blackberry to pass time. With her head buried down, a stranger approached Gena. "Hey miss lady, is anyone sitting here?" Cash asked.

Gena looked up at Cash and answered, "No." Before she could even look back down, Gena quickly looked back up. Cash was a brother who would make any woman take a double take. After seeing Cash, Gena knew that this guy carried the appearance of a man that she could get to know; really get to know…and she hadn't had that feeling since Greedy. Gena smiled while looking at Cash from head to toe in la-la land. However, he wasn't even paying attention to Gena checking him out.

He was too busy trying to get his laptop set up. After he settled himself, he asked Gena was she a model or something.

"Model!" Gena said shocked by the question. Not because she couldn't be one but because she wasn't.

"You're saying it like it's a bad thing," Cash said as he stretched his hand out. "I'm Cash and I'm a photographer," he told her.

"Oh…," Gena responded as she started choking off her latte.

"Are you okay?" Cash asked her.

"Yes, I'm fine. I thought you were trying to be funny," Gena told him.

"Oh, no baby. It's just that you're so gorgeous and I just assumed you were a model because you look too damn good not to be one," he said. Gena was blushing and was very flattered by his compliment. Gena had not received a compliment from a guy in a long time.

"So if you ever think about modeling, or just taking some pictures, then I'm the man for you." Cash didn't even know her name.

"Oh, my bad. Gena," she told him.

"Gena…nice," Cash said as he handed her one of his business cards and told her to call him when she felt like being in front of the camera. Gena gladly took his card.

Soon thereafter, Six pulled up and in the front of the airport door and called Gena. "Hey," Six said.

"Hey Six," she said.

"I'm here. I don't see you," he told her.

"Okay, I'm coming. I was closer to the end by the

# Circles

baggage claim area; but here I come," Gena told him. Six just waited patiently by the door that he parked near.

"Was that your man?" Cash wasn't hesitant to ask because he wanted to know.

Gena laughed. "No. And I will call you okay," she told Cash.

"Aight lady, I mean Ms. Gena," he said. Gena then grabbed her things and then she walked and walked until she saw Six standing by the door.

"Hey Gena!" Six said while grabbing her things for her.

"Hey Six!" Gena said following behind him. After Six put her things in the trunk of his car, he and Gena got inside and then began chatting for awhile during their drive.

They finally made it to his condo and Six told her to make herself comfortable. He left her on the other side of the condo in his second bedroom. His condo was very spacious as it had a living room and den.

Six decided that he was going to tell Chenelle to meet him at the Wildfire Restaurant around noon. This would allow enough time for he and Gena to get ready. He called Chenelle around ten that morning and told her where to meet him. Of course, she was okay with that.

Gena was having a good time just being away from Dallas. Being in a different state was good to her and not to mention Cash because meeting him was icing on her cake. Gena soon snapped back into reality and started to wonder when she and Six were going to have that conversation they were supposed to be having. No sooner than her thought shifted to the anticipated conversation, Six knocked on the spare bedroom door before entering. "Come in!" Gena said.

"Hey girl! I'm taking you to lunch around noon so get yourself together," he told her.

"Hey, that's wassup. So where are we going?" Gena asked him.

"Well, I was thinking about this place called Wildfire. It's a nice place and they serve steak!" Six said while laughing. Gena laughed too. Six then left out the room to let Gena get herself together and he started getting himself together too. When Six was about to get in the shower, Ani called. "What's up?" Six answered his cell phone.

"What's up dude?" Ani asked.

"About to get in the shower right now," Six said.

"Um…you know I wanted to say something but I'm right here with family so I will save that for later." Six started smiling. While Ani was whispering over the phone to Six, Gena came out the room and started shouting, "Six! Six! Are you dressed?"

"Who is that?!" Ani asked sounding jealous. Six hurried and rushed Ani off the phone because he didn't want Ani to know that Gena was there.

So he hung Ani up with a quick goodbye. "Man that's nobody…I have to go. Bye." Ani didn't even bother to call Six back because he knew Six was lying and was up to something. Ani was beginning to get really tired of the games Six played. Six told Gena that he was in the shower. So, Gena went back to the room and start fooling with her hair and make-up.

After Six and Gena got dressed, they headed towards Wildfire. Once they arrived, the waiter seated them at a table for three. Gena was looking kind of skeptical because she thought it was just going to be her and Six having lunch together. "Six. Is someone else joining us?" she asked.

"Yes. One of my friends will be here soon. She's cool," Six told her. As soon as he confirmed that with Gena, Chenelle entered the restaurant. She asked the waiter to seat her because she didn't see Six anywhere, so she thought she was a little early. Six and Gena were on the other side of the restaurant. While Chenelle was being seated, Six looked at his watch and checked the time; it was going on 12:16 and still there was no sign of Chenelle. Six finally called her, "Hey where are you? I'm here at the restaurant waiting on you," Six told her.

"Well I'm here too and I don't see you anywhere," Chenelle said.

"Okay then you must be on the other side of the room. I'll come and get you," Six told her. Six walked to the other side of the restaurant and looked around for Chenelle. Chenelle saw him coming so she met him half way.

"Boy I thought you stood me up!" Chenelle said as she gave Six a hug. Six laughed. Then they both walked back over to the table and that's when Gena and Chenelle met for the second time. As Six introduced them, Gena stared at Chenelle like she knew her from somewhere, but couldn't recall exactly where from.

"Okay ladies. Well I brought the two of you here today because I have some important things to tell you," Six began to tell the both of them. Six told them very little, but enough detail that the ladies knew exactly what happened.

"Greedy did what?!" Gena shouted. Chenelle couldn't believe what she was hearing. She sat and shook her head in disappointment.

"I can't believe this nigga jeopardized our relationship like that!" Gena was still hysterical.

"Your relationship?" Chenelle asked Gena.

"Yeah! Greedy was my man!" Gena told her.

"Wow. I can't believe this. Greedy was a guy friend of mine and he never told me about you until I came back home to visit," she said. And that's when Gena finally remembered where she had seen Chenelle.

"You're the girl that came over that night that Greedy went outside and then came back in acting stupid and shit!" Gena told her.

"Yeah, I told him that he had given me HIV!" Chenelle told her.

"What?!" Gena said. Gena couldn't believe what she was listening to another woman tell her that her boyfriend had given her HIV too. Greedy had been really doing his thing and some serious lying.

"That no good ass muthafucker!" Gena said.

"You know what Six? You are dirty. I can't believe you thought this was a good idea to get us together like this," Chenelle told him.

"Chenelle, I did this for a good reason. We all need to know what were dealing with," Six told her.

"Dealing with…we dealing with your ass! You are the fucking cause of all this bullshit!" Chenelle then walked off and left the restaurant.

Gena looked at Six and slapped the taste out of his mouth. "You dirty bastard! How could you set something

up like this and expect something good to come out of it?!"
Six didn't say anything he just stared out the window with
tears in his eyes. "The only thing that we have in common,
muthafucker, is that we all slept with Greedy and we all now
have HIV.


SIX COULDN'T EVEN look Gena in her eyes. He just looked
off and walked away without saying anything. "You are sick!"
Gena yelled as Six left out the front of the restaurant. Gena
then walked away from the table and went into the ladies room.
Everyone, in the restaurant, stood gathered around like they
were at a big event or something.

As soon as Gena went inside the ladies room, she burst
out in tears. This was such a nightmare for her that she could
no longer even think straight. The only thing that was clear was
that she was in a different state and alone with no one to talk to
there. Six knew he had fucked up and there was no way to clean
up the mess that he made. He hurt Chenelle and Gena which
was truly not his intention. Nothing about the meeting went as
planned for Six.

After Gena calmed herself down, she came out and
went to sit at the bar. The bartender asked her if she was okay
and if she needed a drink. Of course Gena really did need a
drink, so she asked for a cranberry and vodka. After her second
glass of cranberry and vodka, reality of her whereabouts hit her
again and she began to feel clueless of what her next move was
going to be. Then she remembered the nice gentleman she met
at the airport earlier, Cash. Since she had his number it made
no sense not to use it. At this point, he was her only choice
said to herself.

She called Cash and he didn't answer so she left him a
message to call her back as soon as possible. Desperate for him
to answer, Gena called him right back as soon as she ended her
message. This time he answered, "This is Cash."

"Hey Cash, this is Gena; you know the lady who you
met at the airport," Gena told him.

"I remember you miss lady. Are you alright?" he asked
her. Gena was sounding a little shaken up and upset.

# Circles

"No, I'm not. Can you please come and pick me up from this restaurant called Wildfire? Please?" she asked. Then Gena started to cry not knowing what else to do or say.

"Hold on, hold on. Baby girl, what happened?" Cash asked. Gena really didn't want to get into what happened right then because she was still a little emotional.

"I will tell you when you get here. Just please come and get me. I don't know where I am to go ahead and leave on my own," she told him.

"That's okay. I know exactly where you are. I stay a couple of blocks away from that restaurant. I'm on my way." Cash wanted to help her in any way he possibly could. He hurried and rushed out the door leaving the comfort of his apartment to go and pick her up from the restaurant.

While waiting, Gena asked herself why was this happening to her and what did she do to deserve this cruelty. Luckily she had a round trip ticket so at least she wasn't stuck in Atlanta.

Cash didn't waste any time making it there to Gena. He quickly pulled up in his black 2007 Chrysler 300. After picking Gena up she had Cash to take her to Six's place to get her things. Feeling sorry for Gena, Cash offered his place to Gena. He told her that she could stay until she figured things out. That humored Gena because she really didn't know where to begin with figuring her life out at this point.

Heather Jornay Perkins

## 20. TRYING TO MOVE ON

"WHY DO CICI keep calling me? She know I don't fuck with her anymore!" Larenda told Sharon.

"Girl, she still be calling you?! Didn't you break up with her a few months ago?" Sharon asked Larenda.

"Yeah, I did. She was too fucking insecure!" Larenda told Sharon.

"Um," Sharon said. Larenda was bi-sexual. Her last relationship was with this girl named CiCi who looked more like a stud. They were together for about three years and everything was good in the beginning; that is until CiCi started throwing temper tantrums whenever they were not together. She was the real jealous type and wouldn't let Larenda do anything without her.

One day Larenda just got tired of bickering and fighting with CiCi so she broke up with her like it was nothing. From that day forward she told herself that she was going to try and do something different like go back to dating men. She wanted to explore her options and see if that would work out for her.

"Girl, CiCi tripping. She will get over it," Sharon said. Larenda's phone rang again and this time it was Vann. Larenda smiled at Sharon and stepped outside to talk to him.

"Hey!" she answered.

"What's up girl? Tell me something good," Vann told her.

"What's good is that me and you need to get together sometime," she told him. Larenda didn't want to waste any more time with Vann because it seemed as though they had been running around in circles with each other.

"I feel you on that. That's the reason for me calling you today. I was thinking that me and you could catch a movie or something," Vann told her.

"Oh, that sounds good. I'm with that," Larenda replied. She was down for anything the way things were looking for her; anything that would keep her mind off of CiCi and all her drama. It was a nice change of pace to take that next step and try to move on with someone else other than CiCi. And Vann wanted to do the same thing. He was slowly trying to get over Trese. So, Vann and Larenda made plans to meet up at his place and then go to the movies at AMC Mesquite 30.

After Larenda finished talking to Vann about their plans for later on that evening, Larenda went back inside Sharon's house and told her all about their conversation. Sharon was excited for her because she knew this was something Larenda had been waiting on for quite some time now.

After chilling at Sharon's, Larenda left to go and get ready for her date with Vann. Sharon continued sipping on her pink panties drink while watching one of her favorite movies, Juice.

As soon as Larenda left, Tremaine pulled up. Sharon heard a car pull up in her driveway so she got up from her couch and looked out her front door. Now what does he want Sharon mumbled to herself. Sharon opened the door and just stood there with her arms folded.

"What up? I was just stopping by for a minute," Tremaine told her. This time around Tremaine really did need somebody to talk to because, truth be told, he had a lot on his mind.

Sharon let him in because she had never seen Tremaine so calm and serious. After letting him in, she closed and locked the door and then they both sat on the couch.

"So, whats up?" she asked him.

"Man…this is crazy yo," Tremaine said. He was kind of hesitant at first to say anything, but he knew he couldn't hold it in any longer.

"What's crazy?" Sharon asked him. She really wanted to know what was bothering Tremaine.

"This…man…Sharon, I just want to start off by saying that I love you and I always will, but there has been a lot going on with me that you don't know about," Tremaine told her. Sharon could see that Tremaine was beginning to look a little

# Circles

upset and kind of sad.

"Go on Tremaine. Tell me what's bothering you. You know we have been around each other for too long for you to not tell me if it's something important," she told him.

"Yeah, well I've been living with this for a minute now and I just don't want to accept the fact that it's here. Sharon I could be infected with the HIV virus and I haven't been to the clinic. I mean I'm scared of what the results could come out to be. The last chic I was involved with has it and I think that I'm the one responsible for it," he told her. Sharon was shocked and couldn't believe her ears.

"Tremaine…No, Tremaine. Are you sure?" she asked him.

"Yea, I'm sure. I just got involved at the wrong time. Man Sharon you just don't know how much this hurts." Tremaine then got down on his knees and leaned over in Sharon's lap. Tremaine cried that day like he had never cried before.

"Wow, Tremaine I really don't know what to say," she said. Sharon hadn't seen Tremaine cry like that since he went to jail that time for an assault charge. She held Tremaine and cried with him. She felt sorry for him and scared for herself. "Tremaine, now I need to go get tested too. O' my God!"

While Sharon was with Tremaine consoling him, Larenda was about to console herself. It was going on seven o'clock and Larenda was on her way over to Vann's place. He had already given her the directions to his place and it was clear that she had to be on time because the movie started at 8:05.

While driving to Vann's, Larenda had no idea that she was being followed. Her ex-girlfriend, CiCi, had Cheaters investigating her every move. CiCi was still not over Larenda and she wanted to get her back. When Larenda finally made it to Vann's, the investigators captured all the footage that they could get; from the time she left her house to the time she made it there. Before getting out of her car, she made sure she sprayed some Paris Hilton on her so that she would have a sweet perfume scent on her to entice him.

Heather Jornay Perkins

LARENDA ARRIVED AT Vann's front door with her hand on her hip and a pose that was out of this world. She knocked on the door twice before he finally opened it. When Vann opened the door, he couldn't believe how sexy Larenda was looking for him. He let her inside, looked her up and down, and then offered her a seat on the couch so he could go finish getting ready. Vann knew that their time was limited so he rushed and they headed out the door.

Cheaters had the video camera rolling. They captured footage from the inside of Vann's place on to the time they left for their date. They caught the two of them flirting with each other; hugging and kissing before they got into his truck. After they left, Vann and Larenda headed to Mesquite 30 and Cheaters was right behind them.

When they finally made it to the movies, they stood in a line so long that it was almost wrapped around the corner. While they waited, Cheaters met up with CiCi and showed her all the footage that captured of Larenda and Vann. CiCi couldn't believe Larenda was even with a guy. "Now this is them when they were coming out of his apartment," the host said.

"Wow...wow," CiCi said. After showing her all the footage, Cheaters hurried and got prepared for CiCi to catch Larenda in action. Cheaters' security, camera people, and CiCi all ran towards the line where Vann and Larenda were standing. The crowds surrounding them were intrigued with all the commotion going on. "So, this is who you with huh?" CiCi asked Larenda while getting up in her face.

The people in line were moving back to get out the way as they laughed and gossiped. Vann even laughed himself. Larenda didn't want to get into it with CiCi, so she didn't say anything and just started walking away from the cameras.

"So, you ain't gonna say nothing, Larenda?!" CiCi yelled.

Larenda then turned around and faced CiCi. "Girl you a fucking trip! I don't fuck with you no more!" Larenda said. Vann hurried and ran over and grabbed Larenda before the situation became even worse. However, unbeknownst to him, he walked himself right into the middle of it. CiCi hit Vann in the back of his head. Vann had to restrain himself from turning

185

around and hitting CiCi. The security men grabbed CiCi and then the host, from Cheaters, asked Larenda if she knew why CiCi did all of this. Larenda had no comment; it was already an embarrassing moment for her with CiCi having Cheaters investigating her. Vann and Larenda just got into the truck and burnt off.

"So, how do you feel about this whole thing CiCi?" the man asked her.

"Man, I just feel like all the things we been through was just a joke. I got played," CiCi said.

On the other hand, Vann couldn't believe that Larenda was even involved with another woman. "Man that shit was crazy!" he said while laughing.

Larenda looked Vann upside his head like she wanted to smack the mess out of him. "Yeah, I know and it was embarrassing too," Larenda said.

"Girl, I didn't know that you were into women like that! Damn so you be doing it like that huh?!" he asked her.

"Well I was," she said. Larenda was so upset that she really didn't want to say anything else.

When they left the movies, Larenda told Vann to take her back to her car. She wasn't feeling it anymore. The date was ruined for her, all because CiCi wanted to see for herself what she was up to. So, he did and they both just called it a night. After CiCi saw Larenda with another guy, she knew that Larenda was trying to move on and she couldn't be mad at that.

Larenda deleted CiCi's number from her phone as she didn't want anything else to do with her after what happened. Larenda knew she had to move on and just make it be known that she really was trying to do just that.

CiCi told Cheaters that, after making a fool of herself on TV, she was going to move on with her life too and that she had nothing else to do with Larenda. It was completely over between them.

Heather Jornay Perkins

Circles

## 21. THE SHOCKING NEWS

AFTER GETTING ACQUAINTED with Cash, Gena decided
to stay in Atlanta for a few more days. She didn't waste any time
with telling Cash about her being HIV positive. Cash didn't
know what to say to her. Not because she had HIV, but because
of all she had been through and was still going through. He
understood Gena and the situation she was in and was very
glad that she told him about everything instead of hiding it. He
admired her for that. Even though Cash wasn't HIV positive, he
still wanted to have a special friendship with Gena. Gena felt a
sense of relief after telling Cash about the things she was going
through and she wished she would have met him a lot sooner.
Cash was the kind of person that you could confide in and talk
to about anything and not be judged. He was a good listener
and he didn't criticize her at all.

    Gena forgot to call her brother Chase to let him know
where she was and that she was okay, so she called him after
she finished talking to Cash. While she was on the phone with
Chase, she filled him in on what happened while she was there.

    "Hey sis!" Chase said.

    "Hey Chase," She said.

    "Where you at? You missed the party last night. It was
off the chain until that hoe ass nigga Tremaine showed up!" he
told her.

    "He did?!" she asked sounding shocked.

    "Hell yeah! That nigga is stupid!" he said.

    "Um. I guess. But, anyways I'm at a friend's house in
Atlanta," she told him.

    "You're where? Atlanta! Metro run out there too?" he
asked her. Gena started laughing because her brother was so
slow.

    "Yeah boy! You are so silly. Anyway I came here

because I met Six up here so we could discuss Greedy. He told me what happened between the two of them."

"Him and Greedy....what happened? I'm lost sis fill me in," Chase said.

"Well, it's sad to say, but Greedy and Six messed around before," Gena told him.

"You mean to tell me that this nigga has turned on me?!" Chase said.

"Yes, Chase. And Six was the one who gave Greedy the virus," she said.

"What the fuck! Are you sure?" Chase asked her.

"Yes, I'm sure. I heard it straight from the horse's mouth, Chase!" Gena said.

"Damn sis! That's some fucked up ass shit! Damn…" Chase didn't have anything else to say. He was shocked and now he had a lot more on his mind. The conversation lasted a while because he really wanted to know how Gena was taking all of this and who the friend was that she was with. Before they hung up, Chase told Gena that he would tell their mother, and everyone else, and for her not to worry about it.

As soon as Chase hung up with Gena, he did exactly what he said he would do. He told everyone. Their mother was shocked, very shocked, when she heard the news. She knew that she had to be the person to tell Greedy's mother. After Chase told their mother, she tried contacting Ms. G and then Chase spoke with Darren and Vann.

They were both upset with Greedy after hearing what Chase told them. They just couldn't believe it. "So, you mean to tell me that this nigga fucked around with Six?" Darren asked again. He just wanted confirmation on what he was hearing.

"Yeah, nigga! Six told my sister," Chase said real loud.

"Damn that's fucked up…that's really fucked up. Does he know that we know that him and …," Vann started to ask Chase.

"Hell nah! That nigga don't know shit. I bet he thought nobody was going to find out. We need to go pay him a visit fo' real! And my T-Lady went over to Ms. G's place too!" Chase told them just making everything juicier than what it really was.

"Damnnn!" Vann and Darren said together.

189

# Circles

"Just imagine how Ms. G is gunna feel about her son. I mean all that's been going on and now this!" Darren said. Chase, Vann, and Darren continued their conversation and then decided that all of them should go visit Greedy.

Gena and Chase's mother went over to Ms. G's place and she was surprised to see her. Ms. G didn't know Ms. Mathis was coming over. After sitting and chatting for a bit, Ms. Mathis really didn't know how to come out and say that her son was gay and that he was the one who had got it from another guy and then passed it around. "Okay Ms. G, I really came over today to talk to you about something really important," she told her.

"Okay, Ms. Mathis just tell me. There is nothing that can shock me anymore than what I've already been through," she said. Ms. Mathis just knew this news was going to hurt Ms. G even more. So, Ms. Mathis told Ms. G about Greedy and Ms. Mathis had never seen Ms. G look so upset and sad at the same time. Ms. G was so hurt but she tried to be strong. It was too much for her to bear. It was enough that she found out her son had HIV and had given it to someone else and then murdered an innocent girl. But now this. Just the thought of her son with another guy was too much for her to swallow.

Ms. Mathis leaned over and hugged Ms. G as tight as she could and then told her that she would be with her every step of the way, no matter what. Ms. G really did appreciate all that Ms. Mathis was doing for her because she really didn't have to after what her son put her daughter through.

Ms. Mathis then moved away just a little and asked her, "Are you going to visit your son? I think he really needs you right now." Ms. G just looked in a daze. She was hesitant to say if she was going or not.

"You need to go and see your son because he is still your son and no one else's," Ms. Mathis told her. Ms. G was listening and she knew that what Ms. Mathis was saying was true. Ms. G knew that she really did need to go and visit her son and, most of all, she really needed to pray for him. Ms. G had been through so much already in such a short amount of time.

After talking with Ms. G, Ms. Mathis left her to be alone. Ms. G began to think about her daughter, Tracie, and

how she was going to take all of this when she told her too.
Just imagine if the child you raised, as little angels during
their childhood and even parts of their adulthood, changed?
Something, in between those times you taught you were being
the best parent you could be, caused them to change. Now you
feel as if you failed, but you didn't because it was your child's
choice to make the right decisions and you thought them to
make the right decisions. And for all that you had done for
them you are not responsible for their actions. Ms. G felt as if
she was the one responsible for her son's action just because
there was no father figure around. Ms. G blamed herself for all
that Greedy had done.

Circles

## 22. GREEDY'S VISITS

"GETTING HIGH IN the evening and what I got to do; go see this nigga Greedy from the hood that we knew. Ole Greedy from the South, yeah he fucking niggas too! Now that's a got damn shame cuz that nigga is a fool and all of a sudden that nigga's coo coo," Chase rapped about Greedy while hitting the blunt.

"Boy you stupid!" Peaches told him. Chase started laughing and then he blew the blunt smoke in Peaches' face. You could tell that Chase wasn't really taking all of Greedy's mess real well. It really affected him because Greedy was like a big brother he never had. "Why you talking about that boy like that?" Peaches asked Chase.

"Because it is what it is. That nigga done fucked up. He done fucked up I tell ya," Chase said while sounding like Ricky Ricardo. Peaches giggled while standing next to Chase in the bathroom. Chase was looking at himself in the mirror rubbing on his tattoos.

"You need to stop doing that. You looking kind of funny," Peaches said jokingly.

Chase played like he was going to hit her. "Girl I will…" Peaches looked at him like boy do it if you want to.

"Say baby where is my orange Numani shirt?" he asked her. Peaches went to the laundry room where the shirt was hanging up. She grabbed the shirt and then took it to Chase. He was sitting on the couch tying up his orange shoe laces that he had in his air forces.

"Do you have to look like you're going to the club to go visit Greedy?" she asked.

"Girl you know I stay fresh, stop playing," Chase told her as he kissed her on the cheek.

Vann and Darren pulled up in the front of Peaches'

192

house. They sat in the car for a while because Vann was telling Darren about what happened with Larenda. "Everything was going good; until Cheaters came! That shit was so funny dude!" he told Darren while hitting the dashboard laughing.

"Fo' real! Ahhh! That is some funny shit. And ole girl is bi-sexual, damn!" Darren said.

"Yeah, but ole girl that she was dating looked like a nigga. Man Larenda put me in some crazy mess. She's cool though," Vann said.

After chilling in the car, they both got out and went inside Peaches' house. Today was the day that they all planned to visit Greedy. Vann, Darren, Chase, and Ms. G; they all planned to see Greedy that day.

When Greedy's name was called for visitation, he was surprised. Greedy didn't know who it could be since he had not had any visitors in a while. When he got to the window and saw Darren, Vann, and Chase, he was really surprised; especially when he saw that Chase was with them because he was the one that said he was never going to come and visit him.

Greedy picked up the phone and Chase was the first one to talk to him. "What's up with ya boy?" Greedy asked him.

"Man, shit. Just trying to keep my pockets thick and looking out for moms and Gena. You been aight in here?" Chase asked him.

"Yeah, just maintaining, you know. Man I can't even believe that you stepped out to see ya boy. I see you still pimping the Numani," Greedy said.

"Yeah, I got to. But, yeah anyway everything has been crazy since you been gone." Chase really didn't know how or what to say to Greedy about what Gena told him.

"Yeah, I bet," Greedy said.

"Man, say man, look here get this phone, I can't do this," Chase said handing the phone over to Darren. Darren took the phone and Chase walked to the other end of the room.

"What he talking about bro?" Greedy asked Darren.

"Man some shit been flying around saying that you and Six…" Darren couldn't even finish his sentence as Greedy interrupted him.

"Me and Six. Who? What tha fuck is going on?" Greedy asked while getting a little upset.

# Circles

"Man you know what it is nigga! Shit floating around here talking about you and Six giving each other personal attention and shit!" Vann said out loud. Vann couldn't hold his tongue for nothing because it was bothering him to the point he wanted to box Greedy himself.

"Say, say V. Chill out dude," Darren told Vann while pushing him away from the window.

"Say man they just been saying that Six was the one who gave you the shit and I was like nah not my boy. So I had to come down here myself to see if all this was true. Is it?" Darren asked Greedy. Greedy looked really disappointed and upset. When he looked Darren in the eyes, tears started coming down and he admitted to him that everything that they were hearing was true.

After Greedy confirmed that the rumors were true, Ms. G walked in the door. Darren was disappointed and couldn't even say anything else to Greedy. When Ms. G walked up, they all said, "Hey Ms. G…Bye Ms. G." Chase, Vann, and Darren left with a lot on their minds. They never would have thought that the hardest nigga in the bunch would do something like this.

Ms. G took a seat and picked up the phone. She didn't say anything; there was just silence between them for a minute. She couldn't even look at her son because it hurt her too much.

"Mama, I know what you're thinking," Greedy said.

Ms. G then took a deep breath. "No baby. Gerald you have no idea what I am thinking. It hurts me so bad to keep hearing these things about you that I don't want to believe. I've prayed and I've prayed," Ms. G told him while looking him straight in the eyes.

"Mama…" Greedy couldn't even get another word out because Ms. G wanted him to listen to her and what she had to say.

"I know that I wasn't a bad mother to you or your sister. I raised you two right; even without your father around. Now I've been through a lot of ups and downs with the both of you, but right now, right now, all I could do was ask God to help me. Because the Lord knows exactly how I am feeling right now. I'm feeling hurt, pain, and I'm so angry and embarrassed. This part of my life is a total nightmare and not because you have HIV. Oh, no Greedy it's because my only son, my only son, has been with another man," Ms. G said and then she became silent.

"I know mama, I know. And I'm so sorry you had to find out like this. It was a mistake, a mistake," he told her. Ms. G placed her hand over her mouth and a couple of tears came down.

"I know...I know." Then Ms. G hung up the phone and left without even telling her son good-bye.

Greedy saw how his mother was in so much pain and he had to forgive himself for what he put her through.

Within a week's time Greedy couldn't even live with himself knowing that the fact still stood that his mother knew the truth about him. Greedy killed himself. He slit both of his wrists and then he slit his own throat. He already knew that it was the end for him and he had nothing else to live for. He felt like he didn't have a mother, family, a girl, and no friends. Greedy had lost them completely. He was alone and abandoned by the people he cared about the most. The saddest part was that he never got a chance to tell his mother that he was still her son and that he loved her.

Circles

## 23. GREEDY'S FUNERAL

GREEDY'S LIFE WAS measured too short for him. After the
guards found him in his cell that morning, they hurried and
called for the medics to come and take him away. When the
guards found him, he was slumped over against the wall with
both of his hands dripping with blood. Greedy was pronounced
dead at 5:03 a.m. The lawyer, who was over his case, was
contacted by the prison personnel and he had to call Greedy's
mother concerning his death.

When Ms. G heard the news, she couldn't even finish
listening to everything the lawyer had to say to her. Upon
hearing those words, your son committed suicide, she dropped
the phone. The phone hit the floor and Ms. G dropped to her
knees in tears. The pain and hurt she felt was something that
she had never felt in her entire life. She had never lost anyone
close to her, especially a child. Her granddaughters saw her
crying so they went over and gave their grandmother a hug.
The news was just too unbearable for Ms. G. Greedy's lawyer
said Ms. G name several times, but she never answered. He
knew it was breaking news to her so he hung up the phone.

Ms. G had a lot of things that she had to prepare
for, not to mention all of the people she had to inform about
Greedy's death. Before she even got started to tell anyone, she
called the church to get started on the funeral arrangements.
Then she called her family. Everyone was shocked and
heartbroken to hear that Greedy had killed himself. After she
hung up on her last call, she had to see if his sister, Tracie,
could come back home to attend his funeral. She knew that her
daughter was going to be devastated and very upset that her
only brother had passed. Luckily, the line was clear and Ms.
G was able to talk to someone. One of the clerks in the office
answered the line, "County Clerk's office."

# Heather Jornay Perkins

"Hi, my name is Gladys Anderson and I have a daughter by the name of Tracie Anderson housed in your facility. I was trying to see if there was a way that she could come to her brother's funeral. Would that be a problem?" she asked the clerk.

"Oh, I'm sorry to hear that and honestly Ms. Anderson I really would have to look into it for you. If I'm not mistaken, it has to be either parents or immediate family; so I'm sure it won't be a problem. If I can get that information from you, I will call you back and let you know," the clerk told her.

"Okay, please do get back with me my number is 469-221-2223," Ms. G told her. The clerk took Ms. G's telephone number and they ended the call. After she hung up the phone, Ms. G then called Ms. Mathis, but there was no answer. Ms. G decided to put some clothes on and go out to tell everyone, who really needed to know, about Greedy.

She dropped the girls off at the daycare so she could get some things done. After dropping the girls off, Ms. G went over to Wise Fisherman Church to talk with the Bishop and his wife. They discussed all of the arrangements that needed to be made and made sure Ms. G was going to be okay. Right before Ms. G was about to leave, her phone rang; it was Ms. Mathis calling her back.

"Hey Gladys I saw that you called earlier. How are you feeling?" Ms. Mathis asked her.

"Well, this time it's worse than I could ever imagine," she told her.

"What? What happened? Are you okay?" she asked.

"No, no I'm not. My son died this morning and it's all because of me. I did this. After visiting with him and the things that I told him, who could've blamed him for this," Ms. G told Ms. Mathis.

"No, you're not to blame Gladys. You did all you could for your son. And I'm so sorry that this has happened," Ms. Mathis expressed to her.

"I know…" Ms. G was lost of words.

"Do you need me to help you with anything?" Ms. Mathis interjected.

"Yes, yes please. Can you tell all of his close friends what happened and I will let you know about the arrangements

197

# Circles

later," Ms. G requested.

"Okay, I will do that for you. And I am here for you, okay," Ms. Mathis said.

"Thank you Ms. Mathis, for everything," she told her.

"You're welcome. We all have hard times and this time you need to be with family and friends." Ms. G was emotionally overwhelmed; her heart was filled with pain and guilt. She never thought that something like this would have happened to her and her family; especially not to her son.

After Ms. Mathis hung up with Ms. G she started contacting all of Greedy's friends, starting with Gena. Gena was still in Atlanta, Georgia enjoying herself with Cash. Finally, her mind was free from all the drama and negativity that was going on back home. Gena saw her mother calling so she picked up the phone immediately. "Hey mama!" Gena said sounding happy to hear her mother's voice.

"Hey baby! And where are you?" she asked her.

Gena started laughing. "Mama, Chase didn't tell you? I'm in Atlanta with a good friend. And mama, he is so amazing," Gena said.

"Okay, that's good Gena. I can't wait to meet him. And yes, Chase did tell me where you were. I just wanted to hear it from you. Anyway, baby I have some news about Greedy," she told her.

"Oh no. What is it this time?" Gena asked.

"Are you alone, or can you go somewhere where you can be by yourself?" Ms. Mathis asked.

Gena began to whisper. "Is it that bad mama?" Gena got up from under Cash and went into the bathroom. "Okay mama, go ahead," Gena told her.

"Okay, baby, um. Ms. G called me this morning, early this morning, but I missed her call. So, I called her back and she had some really bad news about Greedy."

"Mama why do you always go around the world instead of telling me what's going on?" Gena asked her.

"I'm not Gena. Ms. G told me that Greedy is no longer with us. He is gone, baby. He killed himself early this morning," her mother told her.

"Mama, are you sure? How did this happen?" Gena asked her. Gena was trying to avoid the real situation and what

198

she was really hearing. The fact that her mother was trying to tell her that her ex-boyfriend died was not registering through to Gena.

"Gena he slit his wrist and then his throat," she told her. As soon as her mother said that, Gena broke down and cried. She slowly moved the phone away from her ear and placed it on the sink. She put both of her hands over her face and just cried. Ms. Mathis thought Gena was still on the phone; however, once she realized that she wasn't, she just hung up.

Gena stayed in the bathroom for a little while longer and remained very quiet. Gena thought about all she had been through with Greedy and how much she was going to miss him.

Cash noticed how long Gena was in the bathroom, so he got up from the bed and went over to the bathroom door and knocked softly. "Gena, baby. Are you alright in there?" Gena was still in shock that Greedy was really gone and was not coming back.

She was staring at herself in the mirror when she heard Cash at the door. Gena opened the door slowly. As soon as she saw Cash, she hugged him tightly and then cried some more. Gena knew that it had been rough for Greedy, but she didn't expect him to go out the way that he did.

"Baby...baby what's wrong?" Cash asked her. He was still hugging her as he walked the both of them over to the bed. Gena tried to clear up her face, wiping her tears away as they kept coming down.

"Okay...um. You remember my ex-boyfriend that I told you about, Greedy? Well, he died this morning." Gena started to cry again. Suddenly, she started hitting on Cash. "Cash I didn't expect this to happen to him, not him. I have to go back, I have to go back home," she told him while trying to clear her face up from the tears.

Cash grabbed her hands and lovingly restrained her. "Okay, okay baby. It's going to be okay. I'm here for you. I know it's going to be hard for these few days and I'm going to be here for you. I will get you back home," Cash told her.

"Okay. Thanks Cash. You are being too kind to me," Gena told him while attempting to smile through her anger and tears. Gena then asked Cash if he wanted to come back home

# Circles

with her. Cash didn't say no, he didn't have any problems at all with going. He really wanted to be with Gena because he finally met a woman he felt as though he could trust and he knew that this opportunity didn't come around too often. So being with her every step of the way was his way of showing her that he truly cared for her and wanted to be there with her.

After Ms. Mathis told Gena, she called Chase and relayed the information to him. He couldn't believe or understand why Greedy would do something like that. Chase tried to keep his cool and hold himself together. He called his mother and told her that he would tell the others about it.

Peaches and Chase were together when he spoke to his mother. Peaches was shocked and saddened by the news and she knew that Chase was too. Chase had to deal with this madness if he wanted to or not. He was hurt and didn't know how he was going to tell Vann and Darren. All he knew was that he had lost someone who he truly loved like a brother. After showing out at the jail, he felt even worse because he said some ugly things to Greedy that he knew was wrong. Chase regretted that he ever went up to the jail to visit Greedy.

After thinking to himself, he called Darren and Vann on three way. When Darren heard the news, he couldn't believe that it was Greedy who killed himself and he took it really hard.

"Man, I just saw him. I can't believe...Man how did he kill himself?" Darren asked Chase.

"All I know is that he cut his wrist and bled to death," Chase told him.

"Damn," Darren said. Darren didn't have anything else to say. All he could think about was that he needed to contact Ms. G.

As soon as Darren clicked off the line with Chase and Vann, he called Ms. G. He spoke with her for a while and told her that he would help with anything she needed. Ms. G was very appreciative on how everyone was there for her during this time of grief.

Chase and Vann finished their conversation. The whole time they were on the phone, Vann tried to be hard and seem like he was okay. Nonetheless, he was truly sad and hurt because, even though he and Greedy always had their differences, Greedy was still one of his best friends. He felt even

worse knowing that he chewed Greedy out the last time
he spoke to him when they all visited him in jail. He prayed
that that didn't have anything to do with the reason he killed
himself. Vann felt real bad and he knew he had to call Chenelle
and tell her, but he really didn't know how to. He knew no one
else was going to call her so it might as well have been him.

Chenelle was still waiting on Vann to call her back
from the last time she missed his call.

"Hey buddy," she said.

"What up girl. How you been?" Vann asked her.

"Good. Good," she told him.

"Well, I was going to call you back that day, but I got
caught up in something else. You know things have been a little
crazy around here lately," Vann said trying not to sound too
disturbed.

"Oh, I can just imagine and on my end too. How have
you been though?" Chenelle asked him.

"Man, good. Just trying to get myself back together.
Everything's been cool though," he told her.

"That's good," she replied.

"But, yeah Chenelle I was calling you because
something happened this morning to Greedy. He killed
himself. They say he cut his wrists and bled to death, or
something like that," Vann told her.

Chenelle wanted to make sure she heard Vann clearly.
"What?! Are you serious?" she asked him.

"Yeah," he said.

"That can't be!" she said in a loud tone. Chenelle
went hysterical and then burst into tears. "Vann how could
something like this happen!" she said.

"I know, I know Che. It's going to be okay though. I
don't know when everything is, but I think you should come,"
he told her.

"I am coming. I am…," she said as she hung up with
Vann.

After crying and allowing the horrible news to sink in,
Chenelle pondered over whether or not she should call Six
and let him know about Greedy's death. She knew it was the
right thing to do so she went ahead and called.

# Circles

SIX SAW CHENELLE'S number pop up on his caller ID while he was sitting at his desk. When he answered the call, before he could say anything, Chenelle began to speak. She didn't want to deal with the friendly, yet phony, chit chatting so she just flat out told him that Greedy was dead; the rest was left up to Six. Since he wasn't the type to not show up, he knew that he had to pay his respects. His mother always told him that, even though you and that person have gone through ups and downs, you should always be the bigger person and be respectful.

Six quickly filled out a form for some time off from work and then he told Ani that he was going to be away for a week or so. Of course Ani wanted to go with Six, but Six knew that that wasn't going to be a good idea. He knew that all of Greedy's family and close friends were going to be there and that he didn't get along with any of them. Ani still acted as though Six just didn't want him around, so he took it the wrong way and accused Six of trying to mess off on him. Ani was too damn insecure and Six wasn't trying to hear him at that moment. He left walking out his office leaving Ani with his mouth wide open.

Six went home and got some of his things together, called and made hotel reservations, and reserved a rental car. Afterwards, he went straight to bed because he would need his rest for his trip and potential drama surrounding his past and Greedy's death.

The next day came and the wake and funeral arrangements were finalized. Ms. G was still waiting on the clerk to call her back about Tracie's release for the funeral. While she was waiting, Ms. Mathis called her to let her know that she decided to have the gathering, after the service, at her place and everyone was participating by bringing the food and drinks to her house. Ms. G was more than thankful for what Ms. Mathis was doing for her and her family.

An hour had passed before Ms. G's phone finally rang; it was the clerk. She informed Ms. G that she was able to make arrangements for Tracie to be able to attend her brother's funeral. Ms. G couldn't believe her ears. She was relieved and happy that her daughter would be able to say her good-byes and also see her daughters who she hadn't seen in almost a year.

A lot of people came to the wake on that Friday

evening at Golden Gate Funeral Home; family from out of town, close friends, and even friends from the strip club. The wake was nice and there was no drama at all. Six didn't attend the wake because he thought it would be more appropriate for him to attend the funeral only.

The day of the funeral finally arrived and everyone was at the funeral home to pay their respects to Greedy. Everyone who had grudges against each other kept it to themselves out of respect for Greedy's mother and his family. It was an open casket funeral and as soon as everyone entered the church they were allowed to walk to the casket and say their good-byes. It was so hard for some of them to look at Greedy. Gena was really hurt and Chenelle was too. Greedy's mother was taking it pretty well as she knew she had to be strong for everyone else.

When Tracie entered the church, her mother and daughters were so happy to see her. They were allowed to embrace her for a moment. Tracie's main goal was to say her good-byes to her brother so it was hard for her to focus on the love and happiness she was receiving from her mother and daughters. As soon as they finally let her go, she walked over to her brother's casket and leaned over him in a deep stare. Tracie wanted to absorb every thought and every fiber of his being for that moment so that she could have that last sight of him to cherish for the rest of her life. Tracie loved her brother more than life itself and she found it hard to fathom having to live the rest of her own life without him. But she knew she would have to figure it out and say her final good-byes. After saying her good-byes to her brother, the guards allowed Tracie to hug her mother and daughters one last time before she left.

After Tracie left, the service started. The service lasted for an hour and a half. Six was there but he sat in the back where no one could see him. He tried to remain incognito so that he wouldn't capture anyone's attention.

After the burial, Vann, Darren, and Chase all stood around the dirt that was laid on top of the casket covering it 6 feet under.

"Man, we had some good times," Chase said while smiling.

"Yeah, we did," Vann said.

"Boy, you know you gunna be missed, G," Darren said.

# Circles

After they all said their last good-byes to Greedy, they all placed a white rose on the ground in remembrance of their homeboy.

As time flew by, everyone all met up at Ms. Mathis place for the final gathering. Gena, Chase, Cash, Darren, Vann, Sonya, Chenelle, Trese, Peaches, Tank, Mico, Desmond, and Branden were all in the den. It was like the circle was formed and at least everyone inside that circle knew someone there. Once everyone really took a good look around and figured that they knew someone in the circle, their feelings became mutual because everyone in that circle of friends had been affected by everything that had been going on between all of them. However, there was one person missing.

Six came in making a grand entrance into the den and everyone knew that it was about to be some mess. Six expected for all of them, who knew of him, to despise him. However, everyone looked at him and then went right back to what they were doing. It was as though they had all been through so much within that circle that they were just tired and wanted to put the madness to an end.

Six noticed how everyone looked over at him except for Chenelle. She was deeply hurt and couldn't stand the sight of Six. Since there was no conversation for him in the den, Six turned to walk out of the room. Right before Six left out of the room, Chenelle looked up at him and said, "Six, do you know who gave it to you?"

Six just looked around at everyone and when he opened his mouth to say who it was, Vann grabbed Chenelle and whispered, "Don't you think that this has been enough, Che'?"

"No, no, I don't. I just want to know who," she said out loud. Six thought it was very funny that she had put him on the spot like that. Six was a little hesitant to say, but he knew that the question had to be answered.

"It was LD." After telling them who the person was that gave him the virus. All of their mouths dropped and that's when their circle had gotten a lot more interesting than it was before.

As everyone watched Six leave the house, they were in a silenced shock to hear that the biggest party promoter in Dallas, Texas was spreading the HIV virus like it was nothing.

Branden was especially shocked because he didn't expect it to be LD; the person who had been kicking it with on the low.

While, everyone watched Six depart, Branden held his hands over his face and started to walk out of the living area where they all were. Mico then glanced at his brother and he knew something was up because every time he looked up, his brother was always on his way over to LD's place or he was already there. Everyone else, on the other hand, was clueless to what Mico and Branden knew. And this was how the circle began; secrets were kept and innocent people were innocent bystanders who became victims in the next chapter like a book.

# Circles

Ms. Heather Jornay Perkins is an Aries rising daughter of "Sunny South" Dallas. Her passion for writing developed upon her graduation from Lincoln High School and entry into El Centro College. While in college, she won her first poetry contest and her prize winning piece, 'Young Black Woman', was placed on poetry.com. Winning the contest on such a real topic confirmed that Heather's writings and topics of interest were leading her down the right path. Staying true to her homegrown roots, Ms. Perkins' debut novel, *Circles*, keeps it real from beginning to end. *Circles* is an exploration of the dangers of casual sex in any community.

Heather Jornay Perkins

www.ingramcontent.com/pod-product-compliance
Lightning Source LLC
Chambersburg PA
CBHW060809120626
46557CB00001B/137